BLACK STARS
OVER MEXICO

BLACK STARS
OVER MEXICO

SUSAN EVANS MCCLOUD

Published and Distributed by:

PUBLISHING & DISTRIBUTION

Granite Publishing and Distribution, L.L.C.
270 South Mountainlands Drive
Orem, UT 84058
(801) 229-9023

Second Printing, August 1997
ISBN: 1-890558-02-8

Front cover artwork by Robert T. Barrett
Back cover photo by Glen Ricks Photography
Production by: *SunRise Publishing, Orem, Utah*

for my sister
JEANNINE GEORGE
whose deep love for Mexico has given me
an appreciation of its land and its people—

and for
HARVEY CALL
whose love of the Colonies and whose
colorful, sensitive descriptions have awakened
a fascination and respect for them in my
own heart.

.

Chapter One

It was a wild and abandoned race from the very beginning. Six of us boys met just after sunrise, when the Mexican sun spilled over the low brown hills like rich yellow butter. It was our first race of the spring and the horses were frisky. I suppose you could say we were frisky, too. Our limbs felt like they needed to stretch and move some. There would be work to do when the sun topped the last hill and flooded the valleys: water to carry, wood to gather and livestock to feed—chores to complete before the school bell rang at the red brick academy. But all that could wait. None of those things mattered. All that mattered was the horse's breath in the still, bright morning, the sun warm on my neck and hair, my fist searching a pocket to add my own loot to the pile that already contained a bone-handled pocket knife, a new tin whistle, three round, smooth cats-eye marbles, some horehound candy and more. I didn't wait to count. I knew it was winner take all: that's how we played it. I climbed up on the back of my pony. I felt him shudder. I felt his taut, pent-up strength like a wound spring beneath me.

We lined up at the usual spot. The course was an old one. From the Mesquite tree it wound through a straight stretch of meadow, then left down into a gentle hollow gully. Another straight stretch, then a scramble up the far side, with our horses straining and panting. We'd run it so many times before, I could feel it inside me. My eyes turned to Almonzo.

When his hand went down I would touch heels to my pony's flanks and the wind would claim us. I waited. My muscles ached. My throat felt as dry as old harness leather. Quick as a bat Almonzo's hand flashed and fell. The six horses bolted and began running in long sweeping pleasure across the field. The course was just over two miles long. A few minutes would tell it. But I felt, skimming over that meadow, as if time no longer existed. There was a wind in my face and a high, roaring sound in my ears. I could have gone on and on like this, forever.

Glancing to my left I saw Spencer Palmer approaching. Lewis Palmer was my best friend and Spence was his brother. His older brother. But that didn't matter. Lewis and I were the youngest boys there, but age made no big difference. It was the course and the horse beneath you, your pluck, your judgment, the ground conditions and the hand chance dealt you: would you avoid the matted roots, the treacherous pot holes, the jagged rocks that the high grass hid? Would your horse keep his footing? Would the slope where your mount took it be smooth and firm, or wet and loose and studded with pebbles?

We were approaching the end of the stretch with the gully before us. Only Almonzo and Willie Stout rode ahead of me. Spencer hung back with his pinto's nose at my pony's tail. Lewis and Wesley Jarvis were in the rear and would probably stay there. The rider I had to beat was Almonzo. My horse was running easily. I wouldn't push him, not yet. There was still the gully, and after the gully the obstacle course where the path wound a tortuous way around ocotillo, manzanita and scrub oak, past standing boulders some giant had tossed from the high peaks above. There one, maybe two riders could run abreast. If you placed too far behind in that lineup you'd never make it up during the final short open stretch to the finish.

We were approaching the descent to the gully when I heard it, a high, piercing call like an Indian war cry but brighter, and edged with laughter. I turned in the saddle feeling my horse break gait beneath me. *Alicia!* How did she know? How had I given it away? I had been careful, so careful this time.

I heard Spence mutter something under his breath, then he bent low in his saddle. If Alicia was here, then the fun was over. My horse took the lip of the gully well. But it seemed I could *feel* Alicia behind me.

We had really a long head start, but that didn't matter. My Diablo was a plucky range horse, really only a pony, standing less than sixty inches tall. No boy here had a horse that could match Alicia's.

With the feel of her bearing down upon us we all went wild. I urged Diablo across the gully and up the incline at twice the pace he was used to. Spencer's pony cleared Diablo's flank, and his nose seemed to hang at his shoulder. Almonzo had pulled ahead of Willie and climbed the gully. I bent low and whispered in my horse's ear.

Inch by inch the gap between my horse and Willie's shortened, until suddenly it had disappeared. I moved so close to Willie that my foot brushed his trousers. For a few moments the two horses moved together like equal parts of some beautiful pounding machine. Then imperceptibly Diablo pulled forward and broke the invisible cord that seemed to bind the two. We burst over the edge of the gully and into the brush. There was no one ahead of me now but Almonzo! I took a deep breath and, as I did, something swift brushed past me, something swift and white and golden. A tongue of Alicia's red-gold hair licked at my shoulder like a flame. I brushed my own hair out of my eyes. My hand was trembling. I wet my lips with my tongue. The white stallion swept past me. He seemed to move almost effortlessly. It could be exciting to watch Starfire run, but not this morning. Not eating his dust. Not watching the girl who rode him toss her haughty golden head and approach Almonzo as relentlessly as she had pushed past me.

I looked down, away from Alicia, just in time. I was heading pell-mell for the clump of ocotillo bushes on my right! They seemed to race toward me, too. I pulled Diablo's mouth cruelly. He veered, but not quite in time. A branch caught at my shoulder and the thorns tore a long red gash down my arm. I hardly felt it. Diablo stumbled into a pocket, a hidden hole. He lunged forward, and I felt my body jerk with his. I grabbed desperately for something to hold onto, but my fist closed over nothing but air. At last my left hand found Diablo's head, then a clump of hair. At what seemed the last moment I righted myself and regained my seat—and Diablo surged forward. Too late. I was staring at the back of Willie's head and his pony's hindquarters! I pushed hard for the rest of the course, but I never caught him. I was third to reach the finish line. That is if I didn't count Alicia—and I refused to count Alicia!

I climbed down from Diablo's back. Willie approached me and stuck out his hand. "You ran a good race, Harvey. If Diablo hadn't nearly gone down by the ocotillos you'd have been second."

I nodded and shook his hand. Willie was an honest, straightforward boy, a little simple perhaps. Non-competitive compared to most of us. That made it worse—he was too darn nice to get sore at.

Almonzo stood by his pony. He caught my eye and his dark brows creased into a frown. "Time to get back, boys," he said with matter-of-fact authority. He paused a moment, then added, "Thanks for the race, Harvey." That was a high compliment, coming from Almonzo. I felt my face redden.

No one spoke to Alicia, or seemed to notice her presence. That didn't bother her in the least, and why should it? She had beaten every last one of us, and that's what she'd wanted. We knew it, and she knew we knew it. She smiled at Almonzo.

"You're getting better all the time. Maybe some-time I'll race you—just the two of us—with *you* riding Starfire."

Almonzo looked up at that statement, in spite of himself. She smiled again, then turned the white stallion and rode over to where I was standing.

"You've torn your shirt, Harvey. Mother won't be pleased. Would you like me to take it with me for Helena to mend before school?"

Helena was my mother's housekeeper who

cooked our meals, did general housework, mended the clothing. I didn't answer her. I didn't move a muscle. "Suit yourself," she said, unruffled. "Just trying to help."

Help! I spat into the dirt with all the disdain I could muster. It didn't make me feel any better. Alicia rode Starfire back down the trail. Even after she left us the air was charged with the tension she had created. Nobody said much. We rode single file back to the starting line. Almonzo didn't even get off his horse, but bent low in the saddle and scooped up the winner's pile. Almonzo's mother was a Mexican beauty, but his father was English. He had been an English officer. He was very thin and taller than most men. Almonzo was dark-complexioned and looked like his mother, but he was tall already, just like his father.

He did one last thing after he retrieved the pile of treasure. He turned his piercing black eyes 'til their gaze fell on me. "She's your sister, Harvey."

I knew what he was saying. I swallowed and nodded. It would do no good to protest, to remind Almonzo that no one told Alicia what to do. No one attempted to control her. She was my sister. That meant it was up to me.

We turned our horses and rode down into the valley. Almonzo's words sat like rocks in the pit of my stomach. *She's your sister . . . she's your sister.* A field lark was singing. The fresh morning air smelled like flowers. I knew at our ranchhouse there would be hot baking-powder biscuits with blackberries for breakfast. But the lump at the pit of my stomach tasted sour. I could still see the look in Almonzo's dark eyes. The day was ruined as far as I was concerned.

Chapter Two

Mexico in the spring of 1911 was an exciting place for a boy to be. Revolution was in the wind, especially in the state of Chihuahua. Porfirio Díaz, who was now an old man, had ruled Mexico for thirty years. He was considered by many a tyrant, enemy of the peones and the Indians. Madero, the fiery fanatical little man they called "the Redeemer" had declared himself "Provisional" President of Mexico. He could talk—he had a tongue like an angel. With words and the magic of his personality he convinced the people that *he*, Madero, could create a Utopian state where there would be no cruelty, no poverty, and no persecution. He set himself up in the border city of El Paso, and his cry echoed along the stretches of the Rio Grande: ¡Viva la Revolución!

Madero was the people's liberator, but he wasn't the only one making a stir. There was the outlaw, the bandito Pancho Villa and his Villistas. This spring there were rumblings and rumors all around. Something was in the wind, something could happen right here in Chihuahua.

Chihuahua is the largest state in Mexico and no horseman could ride over it in any direction without crossing land that was part of the feudal estate of Don Luis Terrazas. He was one of the richest cattlemen in the world. The number of his beeves, or prized cattle, was legendary. The story was told that once a Chicago firm ordered a million head of his cattle. Don Luis wired back a reply asking one single question: *What color?*

The peones hated men like Terrazas, who paid those who worked for him twenty-five centavos a day, and was content to let them sleep in hovels and live in hopeless ignorance, much like slaves, forced to buy their chili, beans, coffee, sugar and manta from *la Tienda de Raya*—the company store. There the food the peones needed always cost more than the money they carried, so that goods were purchased on credit, until the peones owed so much of their next month's earnings that they could never hope to break the pattern and be free.

Pancho Villa, the peon, the feared Puma, hated this "Lord of Chihuahua." He did everything he could to destroy him: raiding the Don's big droves of cattle, killing off the *becerros* by the thousands, never striking at the same spot twice, but using the helter-skelter tactics of the *banda,* which Terrazas, with all his Spanish military training, could not combat.

It was something I saw from a distance, but was not part of. I went to school at the Academy, did my lessons, and bought supplies for my mother at the Colonia Mercantile. I took my father's hides to the Taylor brothers at Juarez Tanning, and carried loads of grain to the Stowell gristmill which ran day and night and sent high-grade flour by trainloads to all parts of the state.

There were seven Mormon colonies in Chihuahua. Juarez, where I lived, was one of the largest and most prosperous. The city sat in a bowl-like valley, so that the approach to it from the Dugway was sudden and startling: it looked like a blossoming Garden of Eden, a small bit of heaven.

Our cities were different from the Mexican cities. They were laid out in geometrical design. Our streets were broad, well-kept, and lined with shade trees—black walnut, quince and mulberry. There were small orchards and gardens in every yard. Our houses were built of red brick, most of them two stories high. There were no pool halls in our cities, and no saloons. Smoking was rare, and even the drinking of coffee and tea was discouraged. Our people worked hard and our businesses prospered. We were "Mexicans" by permission, by kind invitation, and we were careful to obey the rules, to behave ourselves. This talk of revolution made our fathers and mothers uneasy. They had worked their fingers and hearts to the bone to build up this place. They didn't want to be forced to abandon the fruits of their labors, to return to the deserts of Utah worn-out and empty-handed.

I sat in my father's study, a small room that stood at the back of the family parlor. It was two days since our morning race, and I still hadn't spoken to Alicia. I couldn't seem to find a time that was right, or the right approach—that was most important. I didn't have any desire to be laughed at. Or worse, ignored with that casual air of disdain Alicia, with all her seventeen years, affected so masterfully. Instead, I did my best to ignore her, to go out of my way to avoid any unnecessary conversation with her. Alicia didn't seem aware of my strategy. She went her way, happy and untouched by my fuming anger.

She was out exercising Starfire by rounding up some of Mother's goats which had scattered through a break in our fence line and gone "visiting" the Madsen's herd further down the road. I had seen her ride out, her long yellow hair flying, not ten minutes before my father called me here. I tried hard to concentrate on the task before me, on the words my father was speaking. "Harvey, you will take care of Mr. Morales, won't you?" I nodded. "I am so pressed for time," my father explained.

He looked hard-pressed. His brow was knit in a furrow of worry. His eyes looked bloodshot, as though he was not getting his proper sleep. I noticed deep lines around his eyes and across his forehead. I didn't know what things my father might worry about. Perhaps it was my mother. I hoped not, not this time. But I would not question him; that was something a boy my age would not do. Besides, I was a little afraid of my father. He was a very important man, and he was an old man. Older than most of the fathers of my friends.

He spoke to the man who was waiting, a Mexican who stood with his crumpled, sweat-stained hat clamped in moist fingers. Father was explaining in the man's own language. Mr. Morales nodded and smiled, showing teeth that were white and even. "Sí, señor. Está bien. Gracias, señor."

I sat down. I had done this before, but I didn't enjoy it. I felt awkward and uneasy. I picked up the pen, my father's pen. It felt cool and firm against my fingers. I dipped the point in the inkwell and looked up at Mr. Morales. He, too, was uncomfortable. He raised his eyebrows into a black point and half-shrugged, an apologetic gesture. *Mi estimado amigo*— "My dear friend," I began, to help him.

Not many people in our Mormon towns spoke the Spanish language more than they had to in order to get along. My father was an exception; he spoke like a native. I, too, spoke the language well. It came easily to me. When my father saw this he began working with me. By the time I was twelve I could not only speak and understand Spanish, I could write it. Sometimes I copied records and accounts for my father, and sometimes I wrote letters, at times letters that concerned my father's business, but more often letters such as this one today.

Many of the natives like Mr. Morales came to my father when they needed an important letter written. Perhaps a baby had been born or someone had died, or a son had distinguished himself, and they wanted to tell it. Many of them could neither read nor write. Even those who could did not possess the skill of my father. Few white men, or *gringos,* would have done such a thing. My father was different. The people trusted him. He was the white chief, the *jefe gringo*— bishop of the Mormon ward. But it was more than that. There was something about him, something that made them feel trusted in return.

So I was here today in his place, the son of the *jefe*. I wrote carefully. I would do my best for this man and my father. I knew I had the name of Joseph Young Hales to protect. I finished the letter and handed it to Mr. Morales. He signed his name. He didn't even ask me to read it back to him. He had assigned to me the same trust he gave my father. I could see it in his eyes when he shook my hand.

I walked with him to the side door; he would not use the front one. He paid me nothing. My father refused to be paid. Mr. Morales, I knew, would find his own way to repay us: a fresh side of pork left on our doorstep some night, a bright shawl or serape made by Mrs. Morales, or a festive piñata filled with small nuts and candies.

I watched him ride away on his stocky mule. It was too late now to go fishing with Lewis. I walked back through the kitchen and cut a thick slice of bread from a new loaf, still warm. I would do my studies. That would please my father when he returned. I walked back to my room with a sense of peace inside.

Chapter Three

Helena was the Mexican woman who worked for our family. At certain times of the year—when the fruit and produce were ready to harvest, at holidays or in times of sickness—her daughter would come from the village to help her. My mother did little of the work. People called her an invalid, but I didn't like that word. Aunt Cleo and Aunt Clair said she had a weak constitution and made it sound like some dreaded disease. My father never used either term. He called her "delicate" and when he said the word it was like a caress, like unsung music.

Aunt Clair was my father's sister, but Aunt Cleo was Father's other wife. Of course, all that was before the Manifesto, when the Mormons could practice this peculiar part of their religion openly—before the Supreme Court and the Federal Marshalls interfered and husbands were stuck in prison while wives and children went hungry.

That had never been part of life for us in the Colonies. I was one of the last kids stuck with a polygamous family, true—but it wasn't as bad as it might be. I knew that Aunt Cleo was older than Mother—older and stout and gray-haired. And, of course, I had heard the whispered stories. I knew my mother was much younger than Father's other wives. Because of her health she had borne him only two children, Alicia and me. That in itself was unusual. Most of the families in the Colonies were large. We were different. Some people called us pampered. At least people used that word the way they used invalid when they spoke of my mother.

I thought my mother was the most beautiful woman alive. She had long blonde hair with no gray in it, but every soft glowing shade of light in a summer's sunset. She spoke softly. She never complained, she never shouted. She laughed often, and her laugh had a musical sound. Mother could do anything with her hands: spin, color and weave cloth; make thread, weave fringe and netting; knit, crochet and embroider. And she could paint! On the wall in my room hung an oil she had painted, one she brought with her when she came to the Colonies. Though it hung in my room, it was one of her favorites. Sometimes I would find her there, sitting in the low chair beside my bed, gazing at the picture, her hands busy with something in her lap.

One time I asked: "Do you miss it so terribly, Mother?"

She smiled—a slow smile that was almost reluctant. But she didn't answer. Not really. She said in a voice much like Alicia's, but sweeter and softer, "Mount Timpanogos—do you remember the name, Harvey?" I nodded. "When it is covered with snow like that, lights play upon it. The crisp air is as pure, I believe, as the air of heaven. There is nothing drab or brown or uncertain about mountains in winter, just majesty, Harvey, sheer majesty."

She had sighed, and I asked no more questions. When she spoke like that, and she often did, I could not understand her. I simply smiled back, and the reluctance in her own smile vanished, and we talked together of easier things than the snow-covered mountain.

When my father came in for the evening meal, we were all waiting. He was later than usual. Helena fumed that her food would be spoiled. My mother started from her chair when she saw him, but he shook his head. He went to her, sank to the floor beside her and laid his head in her lap. She stroked his hair, so black, even with the gray streaks in it. When he looked up, he met her eyes and seemed to take strength from them. He stood and took his own seat at the head of the table before he spoke.

"There has been a battle at Casas Grandes," my father said. My mother gasped and put her hand to her throat. Helena, serving the soup, made the sign of the cross and muttered something I couldn't hear. Juarez is only fourteen miles southwest up the river from Casas Grandes. I glanced at Alicia. Even Alicia looked scared.

"Díaz' men defeated the rebels at San Andres and Cerro Prieto," my father continued. "But the Maderistas, with the help of Pancho Villa, have won a victory over the Federalists in Casas Grandes."

What does this mean for us? my mother's eyes asked. I wanted to ask the question myself. Perhaps Father didn't know the answer. If he did, perhaps he would not tell us anyway. A real battle right here in Casas Grandes, with men shooting each other, with blood and death! I couldn't imagine it, no matter how hard I tried. In all my fifteen years I had never seen a man shot—I had never seen anyone die.

My father finished his soup and pushed back the

bowl. Helena brought a plate filled with food. He began to eat it. "There is a meeting with some of the brethren tonight," he said. My mother nodded. "Don't worry yet, Leah," he added gently. Then he smiled across the table at my mother. "Let's not make ourselves miserable where there may be no need."

He pushed back his chair and rose from the table, then walked over and kissed my mother goodbye. "I shall be home early," he whispered. "I promise."

She put her hand over his. "Take care, Joseph."

He walked out of the room, and it seemed to me that he didn't look tired and old at all. His eyes were bright and alert, and he walked with purpose. I wondered to myself how that could be. Didn't fear make him feel tight and breathless inside? Didn't he feel like he wanted to run away?

Chapter Four

On May ninth and tenth Madero's men took the city of Juarez, defeating the government troops led by Juan Navarro. Villa and Obregon wanted to execute Navarro, but Madero only had him deported to El Paso. We talked about the battle at school, and little else. Wesley Jarvis told gory stories about Villa.

"He tortured Mestas, the saloon keeper," Wesley said as though he were boasting, or something.

"I heard he caught the cannon balls with his bare hands," Willie added.

"Of course, he didn't catch cannon balls," Spencer Palmer scoffed. "No man can do that."

"But he tortured people," Wesley insisted. "That part is true. They tell stories about him because he's a legend—a legend right under our noses, right here in Chihuahua!"

I thought about it as I sat at my lessons; I couldn't help it. There were only twenty-five hundred men in Madero's army—led not only by Mexican generals. There was an American captain they called "The Dynamite Devil" and another they labeled "The Fighting Jew." There was a Frenchman and an Italian Colonel, and a famous general who had fought in South Africa. Why had they all gone to war in Chihuahua? Why had they risked their lives for this cause?

Spring was sweet, and the nights were long and warm now. After chores were done, we boys gathered and played games as long as we dared, until our

parents called us, or 'til some father pried us apart
and sent us along to our separate houses. Sometimes
it was *Pom, Pom, Pull Away, Stink Base,* or *Steal
Sticks.* The night after the great battle of Juarez we
played *Run, Sheep, Run.*
We chose captains for each team: Almonzo and
Wesley. It might seem strange that a boy Almonzo's
age would still play *Run, Sheep, Run* with a bunch of
little kids. Eighteen is a long way from fifteen, much
more than just three years—especially in Almonzo's
case.
But Almonzo always let us talk him into it, one
way or another. Maybe because there were so few of
us to start with. Maybe because he had that sense of
family so unique to Juarez. Or maybe just because no
one could whip us into a team the way he could; even
natural-born leaders need someone to lead.
We drew the usual lots to decide which team
would be lambs, which wolves. Wesley drew wolves.
He was sneaky and cunning, but not really brave as I
thought a wolf ought to be. I knew Wesley would
never choose me. Almonzo chose me. I was the second person he chose. That was an honor. Since the
horse race I had gained status with him.
We set a goal and the wolves huddled there, making wisecracks and rude boasts to each other. We
sheep followed Almonzo, choosing signals to use.
There was one for *Danger,* another for *Lie Low,* and
yet another that said, *They're passing, get ready to
run!* Then at a move of Almonzo's hand we scattered,
Lewis and I running side by side together.
Nowhere, my mother says, is the moon so full,

the stars so near, the sky so velvety soft as in Mexico. I felt that night's softness settle about me, like a shield, like an extra skin, smooth and polished. I ran, throwing my head back, tasting the air. Lewis waved and veered off to my left. He was probably heading for McClellan's ramshackle barn. I didn't want that. I didn't want to be shut in from the night and the stars.

I passed old haystacks, bent and twisted in shadow. I ran on 'til I reached the river bed. Here there were stumps and half-fallen trees to hide me. I worked my way back into the shadowy stillness. A dark shape burst past me, blotting out my light. I heard a short whistle, the signal for *Lie Low*. I crouched down on my haunches. I could smell the rich river mud. I could hear the water as it lapped in a sing-song rhythm against the shore. I stayed low 'til my muscles ached, then I raised myself slowly.

The moon was tangled in black tree branches, half-hidden there. I listened. I heard no voice, no footsteps. A dog howled off in the distance. The sound was eerie and made me feel lonely, but the frogs and crickets kept up a bright chorus around my feet. It seemed as if I had been hiding here for hours. Where were the others? What if the game was over? I held my breath, wanting to hear the shrill signal from Almonzo: *Run, Sheep, Run.* That would release me. I could run for the goal, run with all my might.

I shifted my feet. An owl hooted high above me, a long, hollow quivering sound. I crept a few steps forward. It seemed the dark shadows moved with me. What if a raiding party of wolves found me? They would drag me back to the goal while they all laughed at me. What should I do? I couldn't hold still any longer. The moon still cowered behind the black branches. The owl's cry shivered along my spine. I stepped forward. I felt a hand come down on my shoulder. *Then I had been right!* I was caught. Was it Wesley, Thomas, Spencer? I turned to face him. As I turned, a hand closed over my mouth, hard and bruising, cutting off my breath. I struggled against it with a sense of panic. This was not Wesley! A strong arm pinned my own arms to my body.

I twisted and turned and found myself gazing into a lean, dark face only inches from mine. I screamed, but no sound came out. I was breathing in gasps now. The man who held me was filthy and unshaven and across his middle a white cloth was wound round and round. The cloth, too, was dirty—and stained. In the dim light it was hard to see, hard to tell. But the cloth, I suddenly knew, was a bandage, and the dark stains that spread across it were blood. *A Maderista!* At the idea my mind froze in terror. My legs seemed too weak to hold me up. The man half-dragged, half-shoved me back into the dark trees with him. He pushed me up against a low stump, at the same time relaxing his hold on my mouth. I sat down with a jar and breathed in the fresh air gratefully.

"The Saint Teresa, she has sent you to help me. Gracias," the man muttered, glancing upward and crossing himself. I stared, but in the darkness he could not read my amazement. *I* sent by a Catholic saint to help a revolutionary!

"See, boy?" The man pulled me roughly forward and to my feet, turning my face in the direction he pointed. "See there? There is a cave in those mountains. I go there. You take me there. Now."

As far as he saw there was nothing else to the matter. "You know the way, sí?" I nodded. "You be sure, boy, very sure." He dropped one of his hands to his side and drew out a long blade. The dull metal shimmered. A horrid thought shot into my head: *Had this knife ever been thrust into human flesh? Had it ever killed a man?*

As if he could read my thoughts, the man muttered, "This blade, she know how to slip in between the ribs just right." I felt the sharp prick of the point at my chest. I shuddered. The touch of the man made my skin go cold. "We go. Now." We walked out of the trees together. The man leaned heavily against me for support. Carrying his weight as best I could, I stumbled forward.

It was two miles, maybe more like three miles to the cave from here. But I knew the way by heart; I would know it blindfolded. I set my mouth in a grim, tight line. I must not panic. I must not think about what was happening to me. *Just walk, just set one foot in front of another. Don't think about what the next moment might bring.*

We had not walked more than ten yards when I heard it: two short whistles followed by a long, drawn-out one. The sounds fell into the silence like pebbles into a pool. My first impulse was to call out, to run forward! The man tightened his grip on my arm, and I felt the point of the blade pierce my skin.

¿Qué es esto?—what is this?" he asked. I bent low to answer, not realizing that I spoke to him in his own language.

"It is boys playing a game," I told him. "Follow me. We will go round this way to avoid them."

I turned and he did not resist. I closed my eyes for a moment and prayed wildly that one of the wolf-spies, one of the bolder raiders might venture this far and find us! Or even one of the sheep running homeward, running innocently to the goal—safe! safe!

It didn't happen. There were no more whistles, no shouts, no laughter. We walked away from them into the night together.

Chapter Five

The man's breathing as he walked beside me was heavy and labored. His face was drawn into tight lines of pain, but he kept on going. After a while, my whole body ached from the weight I supported. Each step sent small pains tingling up my legs. But the mountains were nearer—dark bulky shadows against the horizon.

As we approached the mountain the darkness seemed to gather, grow murkier, more dense. I had never been to the caves when it was night, and never alone. Some of the older boys had dared each other, and one or two boasted of moonlight adventures there. I had not reached the point where that offered allurement. I was not really that much of an adventurer at heart. I would rather be home in my bed than on the dark mountain where if ghosts didn't lurk, old legends did. We boys had scared ourselves with those legends since I could remember. Now I was alone on that mountain with a bandito—a desperado! I shuddered. This couldn't be real! If I closed my eyes, would it all disappear like bad dreams in the morning?

We stopped to catch our breath before starting the climb. I looked up. The mountain was swallowed in darkness. In the darkest part of the mountain were the caves, black gaping holes linked one to the other, dank with old secrets and old scars. I must not think about the caves and what I had seen there, or something inside me would snap and I'd start to scream.

For a moment I felt my courage fail me. How could I
do it? How could I go up there with this man? After
we reached the cave, what would happen?
I cursed the ill luck that had drawn me toward the
river. Why was it not Spencer Palmer or Almonzo the
man had found? Almonzo wouldn't quake in fear as I
was doing. Tears wouldn't burn his throat and eyes as
they did mine. For a boy of my age I was quite a
coward. I was disgusted with myself, for I didn't
care. I had no desire to boast of my adventure tomorrow, or lord it over my friends. All I wanted was to
be home and safe!
It took a long time for us to get up the mountain.
We had to pause often so that the wounded Maderista
could rest. He didn't murmur or complain, but kept
pushing forward. By the time we entered the mouth
of the cave I was too dog tired to care what happened. I sank down on the ground, breathing heavily.
The man collapsed beside me. Long minutes passed
with no words between us. At last he raised up on an
elbow and spoke. I could not see his face or his eyes,
but his voice reached for me, like some terrible gloat-
ing evil across the space.
"I am safe now, but I need food and water. Dos
days, tres, my compañeros, my men will come. Until
then, boy, I need food and water. You will see to this
for me, sí?" I made no reply. I sank back into the
darkness.
¿Cómo te llamas?" he demanded. "What is your
name?" Still I refused to reply, or couldn't. Some
thickness had gathered against my tongue. The man
made a short, disdainful noise.

"I know who you are, boy. I know who everyone around here is—it's my business to know! You are the son of the Mormon jefe, Señor Hales. What is your name?" The voice was demanding. I shivered. I was drenched with sweat.

"Harvey," I answered.

"Har-vee," he repeated, stressing the last syllable. "Is nice gringo name. Come closer Har-vee."

I moved closer. I felt very sick to my stomach. And cold, so cold.

"Listen to me, Harvee. You do what I ask, you get no trouble. You take care of me, I take care of you." He laughed, and the laugh was slow and ugly. "You come mañana when it is dark. You come alone. You bring food and water and blankets for Manuel. *¿Counprendes?*"

"Sí, yo comprendo," I said.

"Bueno," he answered. "Is good. If you bring someone with you, if you tell anyone, Harvee, you will die."

He spoke with a matter-of-factness that was colder than any hate I could imagine. I knew he would do what he said and not blink an eye. But he continued:

"You betray me, Harvey, not only you, but your padre and madre will die and the pretty hermana with the gold hair. *¿Comprendes?"* I nodded into the darkness. "I will watch for you, Harvey. I can see the path as it winds up the hill. You know this? Sí, you know this. If you bring treachery with you, I will see it. You don't want to bring death to the people you love?"

It was a question. "No, I don't," I replied. My voice sounded hollow. As hollow as the great hole we sat in.

"I am tired now. I will sleep." He sank back against the cold floor of the cave. I sat in the silence. "Go home, Harvey," the voice spoke from the darkness. "Go home and go to bed. Do not tell your padre. Do not tell your pretty madre. Do not be foolish. I will watch for you after the sun sets tomorrow."

I rose. My feet seemed glued to the floor. I moved them; they felt stiff and heavy. I turned my back and walked out of the cave.

¡Mañana!" Manuel's voice called out of the darkness.

I walked carefully down the steep trail, feeling my way. Even Manuel had been another human being, some form of company. Alone, all kinds of images rose up before me. I thought I saw pumas crouching along the high peaks, their yellow unblinking eyes glowing just beyond my reach. A bat circled and swooped, nearly brushing my hair. I felt eyes watching me out of the black recesses, eyes I could not see, no matter how hard I stared. There were too many things I was trying not to remember! At one point on the trail my foot slid and I lost my balance. I put my arms out and fell with my weight all against my right hand, the hand I used most, the hand I wrote with. A pain seared along my flesh and deep into the bone.

As soon as I reached the flat land I started running. I ran 'til it burned to take breaths, then I would slow some. But I never slowed down to a walk, and I never stopped dead to rest, not once. I was afraid I might not have strength to start again. When at last I rounded the wide curve of road and saw my hou nestled against the outcrop of rock and the stand of black walnut trees my father had planted, a surge of joy washed over me, leaving me weak. I staggered the last few yards. I was home, I was safe now! Why did Manuel's face come back to me? Dirty and streaked with blood, his eyes mean and narrow?

"Mañana." His voice echoed in my head. *Mañana, mañana,"* it taunted as I stumbled forward.

I let myself in the side door. The house seemed quiet. There was no one about to notice me. I wondered what time it was. I had no way of knowing. Perhaps I would just go into my room and get ready for bed. It seemed crazy to walk so casually into my bedroom where everything looked the same as before. *Nothing was the same as before!*

I tripped on the fishing pole I had left on my floor. I kicked at it angrily, sitting down on the edge of my bed. My legs were shaking, my hand was throbbing still. I wanted to cry, but I couldn't. The tears wouldn't come. I closed my eyes, and when I opened them, there was the picture. *Mount Timpanogos. My mother.*

I stood up. My mother would worry about me. I must go to her, to say goodnight. That's what I would have done *before*—when my life was still normal. I walked into the kitchen and splashed water from the pump on my face and neck. she mustn't see me looking like this. I heard Helena. She walked past me carrying something.

"Bad boy," she called out. "You play late with your friends, you worry tu madre. Your mother is sick and you worry her."

It was as if someone had opened a door and a cold draft had hit me. *My mother ill.* I raced to her room. Another voice spoke in my head, a voice I remembered, the voice of the doctor last month when he said: *She is too weak, Joseph. She must not catch a germ and become sick. She is too weak to bear it.* I burst in through the door. She was lying in bed. Her eyes were closed. I sank down beside her. She opened her eyes; they were wide and pale. But she smiled, and her voice when she spoke sounded strong and normal.

"You're home, Harvey."

"I'm sorry, Mother," I cried. "I didn't mean to be so late."

"You look awful, Harvey." She touched my hair with soft fingers. "Don't worry. You worry too much. You are too like me."

"Like you!" I hadn't meant to say it.

"Like me," she repeated, and her smile widened. "Alicia fumes and frets like her father. But you suffer quietly, you keep things inside."

Suffer. Suffer inside! If only she knew—if only I dare tell her, lay my head down by hers on the pillow and tell her all!

"I'm only tired, Harvey. Tomorrow I will be better. You look tired yourself."

"I am, Mother." I leaned forward and kissed her cheek. "Goodnight." I left her room and walked to my own room. Nothing seemed real inside my head. I undressed and climbed into bed. My hand was still throbbing. I closed my eyes. My head seemed to spin and whirl. My forehead ached; sleep wouldn't come.

I climbed out of bed and knelt down on the hardwood floor. I prayed for my mother. That was easy to do. But what help was there for me? What could I do? What could anyone do about the Maderista who slept in the cave?

I walked into the kitchen to get a glass of cold water. I heard voices. One was my father's voice. The other I dreaded; it was the doctor's. The doctor walked into my mother's bedroom, but my father came into the kitchen and noticed me.

"Why are you not in bed?" he demanded.

"I couldn't sleep. I came for a drink," I replied.

He scowled. "You came home late, Harvey. Much too late. Have you done your lessons?"

I shook my head.

"Have you an explanation for this behavior?"

My throat felt dry. I swallowed. My head felt light and heavy all at once. "I fell and hurt myself," I said. "And—I lost track of time."

A slight smile flickered at the corners of my father's mouth. "How did you hurt yourself? Let me see."

I held out my hand. I winced at the pain as his fingers touched it.

"Go to your room, son. I'll have Dr. Burns take a look at this hand when he's finished with your mother."

That was the last thing I wanted! But I did as he said. When the doctor came into my room he seemed very tired, but he was as gentle as he could be.

"It's a bad sprain," he said. "I'll bind it tightly for you, lad, but you must not use it. No games." He grinned. "No studies, no chores. Think you can stand that for a few days?"

I managed to nod. I couldn't speak. This was all I needed! When he and Father left, I sank back on my pillows. No chores, no use of the hand. *Mañana.* Food and water and blankets for Manuel. I closed my eyes. Food and water and blankets . . . blankets . . . mañana . . . mañana . . . The waves of sleep, like thick, smothering blankets, closed over my head.

Chapter Six

School was a continuation of last night's nightmare. I should not have gone to school, but my father insisted. He said I could listen and learn, though I could not write. I don't think he wanted me home and worrying over my mother. If she wasn't better this morning, at least she was not worse. She sat up in bed; she ate Heléna's breakfast.

"You still look awful, Harvey," she said as she tied my shoelaces for me. I cast my eyes down. I didn't want her to see my eyes. She was deadly accurate at "reading me," as they say. I didn't want her to see the fear I was so poor at hiding.

Of course, my friends wanted to know what had happened to me. I steeled myself for the barbs and jibes.

"The little sheep ran home to his mommy," Wesley taunted. "Baa, baa, baa," he cried, scurrying back and forth in front of me.

"You look like a chicken with his head cut off," I told him.

"Won't do you any good to insult me," he shot back. "I'm not the one who ran away."

"Ah, the poor lamb hurt himself," Thomas cried. He had spotted my bandaged hand. I had tried to hide it.

"The little lamb hurt his hand and was scared the wolves would eat him."

There was wild laughter at this. Even the most loyal of my friends couldn't help grinning a little. I saw Almonzo approaching and my heart gave a leap. His was the only opinion I really cared for. Lewis would stick by me through thick and thin; he was like my brother. He was my age exactly, just half a dozen days younger. But Almonzo! That was a different thing. Almonzo represented—well, how could I say it? Age, respect, authority, power. I had come far in winning Almonzo's respect. Would this lose it for me?

"What happened, Harvey?" he asked. It was a serious question. What would he do, what would all of them do if I casually answered, *I got grabbed by a wounded Maderista. He dragged me at knife point up to the old caves.* I could hear the hoots and the laughs! But then I could tell them, *All right, come with me and see for yourselves!*

I could imagine their faces when they saw Manuel. For a moment I wondered if we couldn't storm the place together—six or eight of us boys all at once, coming from all sides! But then I remembered there was only one short, narrow passage. Manuel had a knife. He probably had a gun, though I hadn't noticed one last night in the darkness. He might get one or two of us, anyway. I thought of the point of that knife as it pierced my flesh.

"Harvey?" There was a quizzical look on Almonzo's face. He was waiting for my answer. I swallowed. All I could do was tell him as much of the truth as I dared.

"Something happened," I said. "I had to leave."

"You hurt your hand. why didn't you find me and tell me? That would have made sense, Harvey. We looked a long time for you. The fellows lost the game because of you—" He shrugged his shoulders. I knew that shrug meant: *it doesn't matter to me, but it matters to the rest, and they're all sore at you.*

I took a deep breath. "I didn't hurt my hand until later."

"He ran home to his mommy cause he was scared of the wolves," Wesley cried. "Poor boy. His pretty, spoiled mommy would pamper her baby—"

I lunged for Wesley. My left fist was doubled and ready to strike. Almonzo's arm shot out and grabbed it. I turned on him, angry, wanting to flatten Wesley.

"No fighting, Harvey. You don't need that kind of trouble. If you want him, settle it later, your own way."

"Yeah, I'll even tie one hand behind my back," Wesley taunted.

"Get out of here. Now." Almonzo didn't have to speak twice. The boys broke up and walked off as casually as they could, still laughing together. Almonzo turned to me.

"What's the matter, Harvey?"

"Nothing's the matter!" I shouted. *Spit and tarnation!* I was about to cry. I blinked my eyes angrily.

"Something's the matter," Almonzo stated with his matter-of-fact assurance. "Do you want to tell me?"

Did I want to tell him! The tears stung my eyes. "It's something I have to take care of myself, Almonzo. I left, but I didn't have any choice."

He nodded. He'd accept that explanation—as far as it went, anyway. We turned and walked into the

schoolhouse. Without Almonzo I don't think I could
have gone into that room. With him beside me I
could hold together the last tattered shreds of my lost
reputation, my self-respect.

At recess the talk was all of the brave Maderistas
and their daring feats. The name of Pancho Villa was
mentioned most often.

"The men fought harder for Villa than for
Madero," Tom Randall said.

Wesley laughed. "I like how Villa recruits his
men. If a man is a coward—" He glanced toward me,
"and refuses to join him, he cuts the hombre's head
off and strings his body to a tree."

Wild laughter followed. *What did they find so
funny?* I could see Manuel's face locked in a dark gri-
mace, staring at me.

"These revolutionaries are going crazy," Spencer
said. "They steal cattle, food and guns—sometimes
even women."

"And they kill gringos, just like that!" Willie
added. I thought his voice sounded a little uncertain,
but no one else seemed to notice.

"Well, I hope they come here! We'll show 'em
that Mormons aren't like any gringos they've met
with yet!" It was Lewis who made this wild boast—
not Thomas or Wesley.

"Lewis," I cried, "what a stupid thing to say!
Have you ever seen a Maderista?"

Lewis looked at me with wounded disgust. "No, I
haven't. So what! You think they could scare me?"

"They're not interested in scaring you, Lewis," I

said. "They're not interested in you at all. They'd as soon kill you as look at you."

"Oh, you've got the little lamb scared again," Wesley crowed. I clenched my fist at my side. I'd asked for it! I'd spoken without thinking. I was good at that kind of stupidity.

"Wouldn't you fight them if they came here?" Lewis demanded.

All eyes were on me. I felt Manuel's hand over my mouth. I felt his knife point. I saw the rancid bandage stained dark with his blood. I knew he and his compañeros would make short work of a bunch of gringo school boys. But I said what the fellows expected to hear, and deep down inside I really meant it.

"If it came to fighting, then I would fight! I would fight them with the last breath that was left in my body."

Wesley snorted at this, but no one else made a comment. I walked away from the group and went back inside the building. Their boys' talk seemed childish and ignorant to me. Last week, perhaps yesterday, it might have been different. But Manuel was real. Manuel had made all the difference.

Lewis and I walked home together. We cut through the alley behind the tannery, our usual route. Where the lane narrowed and was clogged with old trash cans and a bank of bushes three boys stepped out from the shadows. I recognized them. Wesley Jarvis, Thomas Randall and Pighead Crane. So the confrontation was to be here and now, at Wesley's choosing, according to Wesley's code of conduct—

which meant no holes barred. It would have been all right with just Wesley and Thomas. I could hold my own and not be utterly slaughtered, even two against one. It was the coward's way to solicit Pighead. Everyone knew Pighead would do anything for pay. He was two years older than the oldest boys in our gang, and a little funny in the head. People called him "slow." It was easy to take advantage of Pighead. For a candy bar or a soda pop at the Mercantile he'd do anything. He wasn't mean, but he was big and stubborn. He could do a lot of damage without even meaning to.

"We'd better run," Lewis hissed at my elbow. I kept on walking. "It's suicide, Harvey, just you and me against them three."

"I can't help it. I can't run away from this one, Lewis." I kept walking, and Wesley just waited for me. After awhile I realized that Lewis was no longer with me. I didn't blame him. I wanted to run away, too. They wouldn't have let Lewis help me anyway. But at least it would have taken one of them to hold him. I had no idea what I was going to do. I kept walking until I was only inches away from Wesley, until I could have reached out and touched his face.

He grinned. "Fancy meeting you here, Harvey. Don't we have a little unfinished business—you and me?"

"Maybe we do. But it's like you said, Wesley— me and you."

"These are my friends, Harvey." Wesley's smile grew downright obnoxious. "They just want to help me, that's all. But then, you wouldn't know about friends, would you? Lewis ran off with his tail between his legs." The three snickered together.

"I'll take you on one at a time," I said. "You first, Wes."

Wesley seemed to pale a little. "Sorry, Harvey, that's not exactly what we had in mind."

I knew it would do no good to argue. If I struck the first blow, I might get in a few good ones.

I struck a smash square on Wesley's jaw, then turned in the same motion and hit at Tom's face. He ducked and my fist grazed along his cheekbone. Wesley fell back with a moan, but Pighead and Tom came at me. I ducked and fended their blows the best I could.

"Get your arms around him," Tom called. "Grab 'im, Pighead."

I ducked low and Pighead stumbled. I took the opening and inserted my boot underneath his foot. He fell hard; he was big and soft, Pighead. But by this time Wesley had re-entered the fray. I felt a flurry of kicks, sharp as tacks at my shins. Why is it that cowards are always kickers? I was angry now. I landed a hard blow in Wesley's middle, but Tom's fist plowed into my nose, and it started to bleed. Pighead's big arm clamped around my chest. Something in me panicked. This was too much like last night with Manuel's arm pinning me and his hand cutting off my breath.

I struck out wildly, with no purpose at all. At this rate the three of them would mash me in no time. Then with a grunt, Pighead broke his hold. A strong hand yanked me out from the flailing arms and legs.

I looked up into a welcome face: Almonzo! Spencer Palmer had Wesley by the collar. Tom and Pighead fell back. "Only cowards fight three to one." Almonzo's voice, usually calm, sounded cold and angry. "I believe this is your quarrel, Wesley." He nodded toward Spencer who shoved Wesley forward. I stepped up to meet him. "That's more like it," Almonzo said. From behind Spencer's elbow Lewis winked at me. I doubled up my fist, my right fist. It didn't take long. Three or four blows, and Wesley was begging for mercy. I was ready enough to give it. My face felt raw. My right eye was swollen nearly shut, and my nose felt broken. Blood had spattered down my shirt from my nose and a cut on my forehead.

At first I didn't even notice how bad my hand was, but when I bent to pick up my school books, I couldn't hold them. There was so much horrified pity on Lewis's face that if someone had held up a mirror for me, I'd have been scared to look in it. I went to his house and cleaned up the best I could. I didn't want my mother to see me and worry. I must save my mother concern at any cost. But at last there was nothing for it; I had to go home. I was aching all over and bone-weary, but with a deep sense of satisfaction inside. To be pushed around by a Maderista is one thing. But to be pushed around by a mean little coward like Wesley is quite another. It eased some of the frustration I felt to know I had whooped him. Wesley knew from now on he'd better not mess with me!

Chapter Seven

One good thing came out of the fight with Wesley. Between that and my hand I had an iron-clad excuse for going early to bed. I looked like I needed to sleep for a week. Trouble is, that's how I felt, too! Mother didn't fuss over me the way I'd expected. She just looked me up and down with deep, sad eyes.

"Don't worry, Mother," I assured her. "I'm not hurt as bad as I look."

"What did you quarrel about, Harvey?" she asked.

I dodged the question. "Oh, you know boys. Lots of things. It doesn't matter." She bit her bottom lip, but she didn't reply. Perhaps she was too weak to argue the point. "Wesley doesn't need much excuse to pick a fight," I added. "But I don't think he'll look in my direction—least not for the next little while." Mother let it go at that, but she knew I was hedging.

One more piece of good luck fell my way. My father didn't come home for supper. He wouldn't be home until very late. In fact, he might even spend the night at Aunt Cleo's if the hour grew too late and it meant disturbing my mother. That fit in perfectly with my plans. I felt encouraged.

I went to my room while the sky was still light outside. I lay down on my bed fully dressed. I needed to rest some. I planned to wait 'til the house was quiet, until it was thoroughly dark outside. I had mentally located all of the things I needed. I hoped I could gather them quietly. If I caused a disturbance, I had no idea what excuse I could make.

I didn't hear the door open. I didn't hear footsteps. I didn't hear anything 'til Alicia coughed. I opened my eyes. She stood beside my bed with a tray in her hands, looking as near to silly as Alicia could look.

"Mother asked me to bring this to you," she said in explanation.

I raised on an elbow to see what the tray held. There was a cup with steaming cocoa in it and a large, frosted cinnamon bun. That was a strange thing about mothers, to my mind. If they couldn't do anything else to comfort their children, they would feed them.

"Put it down on the chair," I said.

Alicia complied. Then she just stood there, with her hands clasped behind her. "Is there anything else?" I demanded.

"I'm not sure, " she replied. Alicia was always straightforward. "You've been acting awfully strange lately, Harvey."

"What is it to you?"

"See, you admit it!" She pounced like a cat on a mouse tail.

"I meant, what is it to you how I act, Alicia?"

"You haven't spoken to me for over a week."

"Six days," I corrected. "Not since the morning of the race. And you deserve it."

"That's the silliest thing I've ever heard!" Alicia countered. "I've as much right to ride a horse and ride well as you have."

"That's not the point, Alicia. Ride as well as you'd like. Just don't butt in when we're holding *our* races. Just don't get in our way! You are good at that."

"If you were real men, you'd welcome the competition. But you don't want to admit that a girl can beat you. That's it!"

Of course that was it, but it went a lot deeper. "None of us has a horse like Starfire," I couldn't help complaining. "It's never fair competition against that horse."

"It is when you have a headstart like you did. I gave you more of an advantage than I ought to have given you, just to be sure. Even then I beat you all soundly—even Almonzo!"

Arguing with Alicia was a useless endeavor; there was no way to win, or even get her to concede one point.

"I'm tired," I told her, falling back against my pillows to prove it. "Just leave me alone for once, will you?"

She hesitated. "It's no fun when you're mad at me, Harvey. I can't help being a girl any more than you can help being a boy. Sometimes I don't like it much more than you do."

She turned to leave. "I'm sorry you got beat up."

I raised up stiffly as though a string were attached to my head and someone had given it an awful yank.

"Alicia! I did not get beat up—it was *I* who beat Wesley. Sprained wrist and all." I couldn't resist adding that.

"Well, I'm sorry about the fight then. You boys are so prickly proud." She sighed. "I should not like that part of being a boy, I'll tell you. It's the silliest thing in the world to fight. It proves nothing, nothing at all—except perhaps the stupidity of both parties." "Did Mother send you in here to insult me?" I yelled.

Alicia shook her head. She looked as close to miserable as Alicia can look; that gave me some comfort. She slipped out quietly.

"Shut the door," I shouted. "And don't come in here again." I knew she wouldn't. I knew now all I had to do was wait for the night to settle down like a black iron mask to hide me.

Chapter Eight

Manuel had not mentioned candles, but I brought two or three along with me, and food as well. It made quite a bundle I had to carry, and my right hand was pretty useless by now. I rolled everything up in the largest of the blankets and tied the ends. I could support it that way in the crook of each arm as well as swing it in my left hand from time to time.

At first I didn't feel afraid; I didn't think about what I was doing. I walked territory familiar to me. There were still friendly lights here and there from barns and houses. I didn't feel really alone 'til I reached the mountain. Here the darkness closed in as it had last night. I paused at the base and looked up into the cavernous blackness above me. *This is crazy,* I said out loud. *What am I doing?* But I knew I couldn't turn around and go home. A man sat up in the cave waiting. It was me, Harvey Hales, that he waited for. If I ignored him, if I pretended away his existence, he would *prove* his existence to me. Of that I was sure.

I began the ascent. My heart was pounding. I had an enormous respect for these caves and the secrets they held. I didn't relish the thought of disturbing those secrets, or being privy—however unwillingly— to other-world, unearthly sights and sounds. Some things are better left untampered with. I didn't want any spirits to get the wrong idea. I thought of the lady in her cold silent chamber and my mind recoiled. *Stop it, Harvey!* I scolded myself, but it didn't help much. My legs felt no more solid than mashed potatoes or the soft squishy mud along the lower river bottoms.

It took most of my energy and concentration to handle the climb and support my unwieldy burden at the same time. I was surprised to look up and see the gaping mouth of the cave before me. I slowed. Should I call out? Was Manuel still there?

"Harvey Hales? Is that you?" It was Manuel, all right. I took the few remaining steps that would bring me within the enclosure. There is a huge outcropping of rock at the mouth of the cave that serves well both as camouflage and protection. Manuel was huddled behind this, a shivering, miserable pile of bones and flesh. I dropped my bundle.

"Is good you come, Harvey."

"Are you ill?" I asked.

He laughed a short laugh. "Shot up and ill, cold and hungry! It is the way of life for a revolutionary, sí?"

I untied the blanket and drew out the items I'd brought him. His head was sunk down on his chest; he hardly glanced over to see what I was doing. As soon as I found the matches I lit a candle. He started when he saw the flicker of light, then he looked me up and down, his black eyes hard and appraising.

"What happened to you, boy?"

I had forgotten my swollen eye and the blue-black bruise that was growing beneath it, not to mention my bandaged right hand.

"What's the matter, gringo, you run into a Villista?" He laughed at his own joke.

"You don't look so beautiful yourself," I retorted, without thinking.

He laughed at this, too. "You are right, you are right," he conceded.

"Here. You might feel better if you eat something." I unwrapped the cold chicken and rolls I had brought from Helena's cupboard, thinking of the rage she'd be in when she discovered them gone. Manuel fell ravenously upon the food, tearing off big chunks and pieces, stuffing them into his mouth with trembling hands, making gutteral sounds in his throat that were disgusting. *Like an animal,* I thought, as I watched him. Once he looked up and motioned for the water jug. I handed it to him, and he guzzled the cool liquid, a thin stream running down his chin and into his beard, making small spots against the filthy gray cloth at his middle.

"You need that bandage changed," I said. "You need a doctor."

He swore at my suggestion. "No doctor will touch Manuel," he cried, half-fearful, half-boastful. "Doctors kill more men than they cure. I can take the pain. The wound—" He patted a spot on his belly. "The wound—she will heal in time." He grimaced; pain was written all over his features. "It takes more than a cur's bullet to kill a Villista. ¿Sí?"

"Sí," I replied.

Manuel fell back with a moan. "I will live now." It was a statement. I think he believed it, but I wasn't sure.

I spread one blanket carefully along the cave floor. "Lie here," I instructed. "This damp ground won't help your wound heal." He grunted. "Lie here, Manuel," I repeated. "The damp ground will give you pneumonia, and pneumonia will kill you before that wound has a chance to do the job."

He opened his eyes and looked me over again, but he moved to the blanket. He half-rolled, half-crawled to the blanket, that is. I suppose I could have done something to help him. But the idea of touching him made my already-unsettled stomach flip-flop uncomfortably. He was so filthy I couldn't tell what was grime, what was blood. His cheeks were sunken and covered with unshaven stubble. His beard—I hated to think what lived in his beard. His hands were black with dirt I suspected would never succumb to a mere human washing. Altogether he was a pathetic, repulsive sight.

As he rolled about to settle himself on the blanket, I noticed something on the cave floor beside him. It looked like paper. I bent to pick it up. "What have you there?" he demanded fiercely as my fingers touched it. I left it lying.

"I don't know," I said. "Some paper. You must have dropped it."

He tried to roll and move so his hand could reach it. I thought: *Let him struggle. It will serve him right.* Then I felt sorry suddenly for my bad feelings. "I'll get it for you," I said, and handed the folded paper to him.

He grunted and peered at it carefully, turning it over in his hands once or twice. He moaned softly under his breath: *Mi querida esposa.*

"What?" I asked. I was sure I had not heard him right.

"Is a letter," he said. "To me. From my wife." He spoke the words with obvious pride. I had heard that tone before in my father's office, by men who boasted of their little prowess with words. My father never laughed at their boasting, nor did anything that might wound that pride.

"What does she say?" I asked. He stared back at me blankly. "Your wife. What does she say in the letter?"

He bit his mustache and stared down at his hands for the longest time. At last he spoke. "I don't know," he mumbled. Then he quickly added, "I have not read it. A man fights and eats and sleeps." He grimaced. "And gets shot. He has no time to read."

I knew this pattern, too. I said, holding my breath, "I'll read it for you, to you—that is, if you'd like."

Again Manuel took a long time making up his mind. I could see the hunger creep into his eyes— then a puzzled expression.

"*You* read the letter?" he cried. "Gringo boy no comprende Español!"

I reached for the letter. He let me take it. I unfolded it rather gingerly. It was dirty, especially where the paper had crease lines. It was thin and worn in spots. I figured it must have traveled a long time in Manuel's saddle bag. There was a date and the name of a town in the upper corner, a town a long way from Colonia Juarez.

I looked at the letter in my hands and hesitated. The letter was very flowery, very personal. Should I read it out loud?

"What you doing, boy?" Manuel growled. "You

don't read the Spanish. Give my letter to me." He reached out a hand, but I took a step backward. *"Mi amada esposa, ..."* I began. It was difficult reading. The letters were faded in spots, and the light was poor. I glanced at Manuel. He lay transfixed, gazing up into the lost recesses of the cave's high ceiling. I don't know what he saw in the darkness there. But María's words drew pictures in my own mind. I'm sure they drew many more pictures for Manuel as he listened.

"My dearest, my handsome Manuel. You are so far from us. But myself and the little ones, we do not forget. Every morning and every night we pray for your safety. I show the baby your picture every day. She must not forget what her papa looks like.

"Rosita can not only walk now, she runs and skips. Her brother teaches her to throw sticks for the puppy to fetch back to her. She sits on my lap and sings pretty songs—I wish you could hear her.

"Juan does the work like a man and never complains, though I know that his lame leg often hurts him. He is strong and brave like his father, I tell him. Juan is proud to think his father is a lieutenant in Villa's army. I, too, feel pride—but I also feel fear.

"Lucinda can make tortillas as good as my own, perhaps even better. She is nearly a woman—you would not recognize her. You would be pleased by her beauty, my love, and her modest ways.

"We miss you, Manuel, we are sad without you. There is no light in my heart, even though

*the sun rises each day. I pray the Saints will
somehow guide this letter to find you. I kiss the
letter, but it is your lips I long for. Be well,
Manuel, do not die. Come back to your little ones
and the wife who loves you.*"

The cave was too silent after my voice stopped. I
turned away and began to reposition the things I had
brought. "There is chicken left here, just a little," I
said very loudly. "And rolls. And water, of course,
and two more candles, and some of Helena's
special—"

I stopped. I was saying too much. I sat still. The
candle flame moved in the unseen drafts of the cave's
cold air. I thought how good a fire would be to warm
my stiff feet and fingers. The candle was just a little
light, but it cast long shadows, weird tongues that
licked the cave wall and would not be still. High
above I could hear the small sounds the bats made. I
refolded Manuel's letter carefully. I walked over to
where Manuel lay in his pocket of silence.

"Here is your letter," I said. "Your wife writes
well. You must be proud of her." I don't know why I
said such a thing as that. But it *was* a rare thing, I
knew, for a Mexican woman from a small village to
have such fine writing as I had read, and to express
herself as well as María.

There was no movement, no sound from Manuel.
"I am going now," I said. Still nothing. I turned and
walked to the mouth of the cave.

"*Mañana.*" The voice was Manuel's, but it
sounded different. "Do not forget, gringo boy."

"*Mañana,*" I said and walked out of the cave
without looking backward.

Chapter Nine

I made my way home from the cave without incident. But I was nearly too exhausted to get ready for bed. I knew I did not dare sleep in my clothes—not these clothes. I folded them and stacked them carefully under my bed. I was asleep before my head reached the pillow, and Helena had a hard time shaking me awake in the morning. My face was stiff and my knuckles raw from the fight with Wesley. The muscles in my legs ached. Even my arm muscles ached from the bundle I'd carried. Doctor Burns was waiting when I walked into the kitchen.

"Let me take a look at that hand of yours, young man," he said.

I must have appeared as reluctant as I felt. He chuckled. "Your mother asked me, and we'd both like to please her, now wouldn't we?" I relented and held out the hand for him to examine. He shook his head several times. He didn't seem to like what he saw.

"You're pluckier than you look, Harvey. Not many boys would go into a fight with a hand like this. Smarts some, doesn't it?"

I nodded. He spread a gooey medicine on it and wound it in a clean, tight bandage, repeating his instructions of the other night and adding one or two. He poked around my swollen eye a little, and dabbed it with some awful-smelling liquid that stung like the dickens. I was happy for the excuse of school to slip out of his clutches.

By mid-morning I couldn't keep my eyes open.

I kept nodding over my books until Lewis poked me awake again. There was new fuel to feed the fires, new stories to tell. The revolutionary soldiers were feeling their oats, ranging farther and farther, needing more food and money, wagons and guns to sustain them. We were too close to hope to escape our share of the trouble. Some of the stores in Dublan had been raided last night, and the hardware store shot up pretty badly. I listened to the stories wide-eyed. It could have been Manuel—it might be Manuel's men my friends were discussing.

"How would you like to run into Pancho Villa himself?" Willie crowed. I hadn't seen anything of Tom and Wesley They'd make themselves scarce for a day or two anyway. Their absence gave Willie and some of the others a chance in the spotlight. Willie enjoyed having all eyes glued on him now.

"He showed up at a house in Dublan last night."

"I don't believe it," I said. Just what Willie wanted.

"Yep, it's true. Stealin' everything he set eyes on. The wife was a pretty young thing—Villa has an eye, you know, for the women."

"I didn't know," I interjected. "How do you know, Willie?" Willie was growing angry with me for spoiling his story.

"This is serious, Harvey. What if it was your mother? What if it was Alicia he put his arm around and said, 'I will sleep with you this night, señorita.'?"

"Is that true? Is that what he said?"

"Heck, Harvey, don't be so naive," Spence Palmer muttered.

It wasn't my mother, amazingly, or even Alicia I thought of. It was María, the face I had conjured up in my mind. Would Manuel do that sort of thing, in spite of María? *We miss you Manuel, we are sad without you. There is no light in my heart*—I felt sick inside.

"It's all right, Harvey. She was a clever little thing. She tricked Villa, and ran to one of the Mexican peon shacks. They covered her with a serape and gave her a baby to hold. Pancho Villa poked his head in, but he didn't recognize her."

The boys laughed at the joke on Villa. I didn't laugh. My head had a ringing sound in it. As soon as school was over I went home and straight to bed. There was a community meeting that night, and I wanted to be there. But I would need sleep if I planned to stand on my feet without falling, much less dance with Lewis' sister, Anna, as I'd hoped to do. Most community affairs ended up in a party. I hoped this would be no exception, although the topic for discussion was grim, and in spite of the fact that it wasn't a weekend.

The evening started out solemn enough, the adults all sitting lined up in chairs, church-meeting like. The girls giggled and minced and whispered in one corner, occasionally venturing out in pursuit of some young child they were tending. We boys walked up and down outside the building, poking our heads in now and again to see if the serious stuff had broken up yet.

"We got enough men to fight if we have to," Lewis said.

"Yeah, most of us boys are good shots, too," Willie added. "They'd better not try spoilin' *our* fields or stealin' *our* cattle."

"That's right, they better not try pushin' us Mormons around like they do the other gringos."

On and on, around and around the talk went, in the same worn out circles it had all week.

"That's not what our fathers are talking about doing!" I threw in. There was instant reaction.

"They want to give up and run away!" Lewis cried. His tone was disgusted.

"I've never been in Utah before," Willie said. "This is home to me."

That's exactly how I felt. I knew Utah was Zion, I knew the prophet was there, and Mount Timpanogos. I wondered suddenly how my mother felt about it. Would she be glad to turn her back on this foreign country, in spite of the soft velvet nights laden with stars? Had this become home to her? Or was she still a wayfarer? My father, I knew, had much invested, not just in a physical or a financial sense. He had built a dream with his life's blood, and it's much easier to kill a man than it is a dream, or to separate the two while the man's still living. For a moment I thought of Manuel. What was his dream? Was it a good dream, worth the sacrifice he was making? Or would it only destroy him in the end?

At last we heard through the open window the strains of a banjo and Brother Dobson's violin tuning up. I sauntered casually back in with Lewis. I spotted Anna across the room. She smiled at me. I don't like many girls, but Anna's the prime exception. Maybe

because I'd known her before, when she was a child,
before she became more girl than person. Of course,
that's not a foolproof theory, because I'd known
Alicia the same way. I couldn't honestly say I dis-
liked Alicia. She just made me uncomfortable, which
was maybe worse when you got right down to it.
Encouraged by Anna's smile, I crossed the room
to her and asked for the first dance. The band was
already playing, and the floor was filling fast. My
father had disappeared; he'd be working still.
Especially as Mother wasn't here to join in the festiv-
ities. This was the Mormon way! Dance and sing in
the face of the worst troubles. Trust in the Lord—but
do it rejoicing, no matter what.
The music beat on and the caller cried out: "Bow
to your partners." No dance except the square dance
was permitted here. Some of the younger folk did
their best to sneak in even an occasion quadrille or
waltz. There was no budging; not the slightest give!
But the Scotch reels and French Fours were pretty
exciting to my way of thinking.
"Ladies change" . . . "Right and left four" . . . I
did my best to follow instructions and yet get as
many glances in at Anna as I could. She has white
skin, blue eyes and black hair like a storybook
princess and the most delicate, perfect hands and feet.
She can look like a vision—something that might
break if you touch it. But she has a laugh that is as
down to earth as warm apple pie. With Lewis and
Spencer and her other brothers, she's learned how to
handle herself around boys. She is the kind of girl
you can feel at ease with. The fairy-tale part is there,
but it somehow never gets in the way.

I'd left early for the dance and hidden my cache
of supplies for Manuel half a mile away, so l would-
n't need to walk clear back home for them. But that
also meant I'd have to leave early. I had mixed emotions concerning that. Leaving early meant I'd be
back home at a decent hour and not wake up a pain-
riddled zombie again. On the other hand, there was
dancing with Anna. Three dances I figured—maybe
four. That was barely a taste. I could have danced
with Anna Palmer 'til my feet fell off or the moon
burned out of the sky.

During the second dance disturbing things started
to happen. I looked casually over at the set of dancers
next to mine and nearly tripped over my feet I was so
astounded. Almonzo was dancing with Alicia, all
mooney-eyed! If I hadn't seen it for myself, I'd have
never believed it. I watched as closely as I dared and
keep up my own steps. He smiled at her often, and
when he took her hand, there was a certain gentleness
I had never seen in him. This was something I didn't
understand. Almonzo was no hypocrite, that was for
certain. What had changed him toward Alicia? I
would have said she drove him wild with her saucy
ways. Almonzo was old enough and then some to go
courting. Could it be Alicia who took his fancy? I
was confused, and I didn't like the feeling. Not one
thing in my life seemed stable or untouched by the
chaotic change that the very air seemed charged with.

After the third dance Anna and I sat down for a
glass of punch, and the old aunts spied us. I did my
best to ease out of their way but didn't quite make it.
Both Aunt Cleo's and Aunt Clair's children had

grown up and escaped long ago. But they still itched to practice their motherly wiles on someone. Alicia and I were the natural candidates, I'm afraid. Mother faithfully and dutifully invited them to supper every Sunday, so they hoarded up their scraps of knowledge about us to use whenever they might. Tonight was one of those occasions they most enjoyed.

"Here's Harvey. Just look at his poor, dear face," Aunt Cleo began, cluck-clucking. That was a rather creepy thing about them—they never spoke directly to anyone. They spoke around them, about them, as though the person they were addressing had become suddenly deaf and invisible at the same time. Aunt Clair took her turn next.

"Well, he needs more tending. Boys his age take sorry care of themselves."

Anna put her little hand up to her mouth to stifle a smile. She could have laughed outright, but she'd never do that.

"Yes, and with sweet Leah an invalid, what can she do?"

I rolled my eyes and decided to be rude if I had to. But Aunt Cleo grabbed my arm in an iron-like vise. There was only one way out, and it made me angry because it would cut off the chance of one last dance with Anna.

"You're both right," I said. "I'm going home now. Straight home to bed. I don't feel well at all."

Anna gave me a puzzled look that went right to my heart.

"That's a wise thing for the boy to do," Aunt Cleo cooed. "That will please his mother."

I stood up to emphasize my point. Aunt Clair dug frantically in the big black purse she carried. "Harvey must take a bottle of our remedy with him, Cleo. It's freshly made. He must take it four times a day, no less, and a nice big spoonful. No scrimping!"

She found the bottle and handed it to Cleo as if it were made of gold, or contained an elixir of the gods. Aunt Cleo reached for the bottle and in so doing let go of my arm. I grabbed the precious bottle out of her hands.

"Thank you both," I gasped. "That's most kind of you. I'll give your best regards to Mother."

"That's quite thoughtful of Harvey," Aunt Clair began. "He's a good boy at heart. A little inclined to—"

I didn't hear what I was inclined to. I grabbed Anna's hand and made a hasty retreat. Not until we were safe in the farthest corner, on the other side of the room, did I slow my pace. Anna looked up at me with wide, beautiful eyes.

"Do you really have to go, Harvey?"

I came so close to weakening then that it wasn't funny. Only the knowledge of Manuel lying waiting for me in the cave stiffened my will.

I deposited her with some of her friends and walked out of the building. The windows threw long wedges of yellow light across the dark yard. The muted music sounded as though it came from far, far away. I glanced in through the window. It looked so cheerful, so cozy and warm inside. The faces of the people were open and happy, cleansed of all worry, as the face of the earth is cleansed by a good spring rain.

Already I felt a sense of no longer belonging, having no place in their carefree company. The burden of what I was doing fell on my shoulders, much as the large forkloads of hay, when we toss them, thud against the bare, unprotected wood of the wagon bed.

I turned to leave; but not before I saw it. Wesley Jarvis stood before Anna, a wide grin plastered across his face. I knew he was asking her for a dance, the weasel! He'd hardly waited until my back was turned!

An almost irresistible urge flooded all my senses, and I half-turned in response to it. All I wanted right now was to pulverize Wesley! Nothing else mattered, not even the cave and Manuel. Then I realized what was happening before my eyes, and I froze to watch it.

Anna was shaking her head very slowly. Wesley took a step closer, persisting. Anna demurred, but Wesley wasn't one to be put off, even by a lady. He had no sense for that sort of thing. His kind never does. Spence Palmer walked up behind Wesley. I could just imagine what he was saying, though from out here I couldn't even see his mouth move. *She said no. She doesn't want to dance with you, Wesley. Leave my sister alone and hightail it out of here.*

It was some satisfaction, I admit, to see Wesley slink off with his tail between his legs, as the expression goes. It was more satisfaction yet to see Anna walk dream-like to one of the tall, square windows and gaze woefully into the empty night. With that image in my mind I turned from the window and set my face in the direction of the caves.

Chapter Ten

As if the aunts and the medicine and leaving Anna weren't enough, I couldn't find my cache of supplies when I went to get them. I scraped my knuckles and my shins crawling around the sharp, rough rocks. I should have marked the exact spot where I hid them. But I had been in too much of a hurry to see Anna. At last, by sheer luck, I stumbled upon them. By the time I'd dragged myself up to the caves I was exhausted and in a black temper. I'm afraid I took it out on Manuel.

First thing I did was give him the bottle of Aunt Cleo's remedy. He looked upon it with suspicion, but I was adamant.

"It's just what you need," I urged. "It's the perfect cure-all. No germ can survive its company." Manuel unscrewed the lid and gulped down a healthy mouthful. The entire bottle probably wouldn't dent the community of germs that called Manuel home. But it certainly couldn't hurt any.

Manuel smacked his lips. "Not bad, Harvey." Then he drew in his breath as the full effect hit him. "This is strong gringo medicine, " he snorted.

"Good for what ails you," I retorted, borrowing one of the aunts' pet phrases. "Good for you—and help you, too."

I set out the supplies that I had brought in careful order: an old serape, two jugs of fresh water, three cold beef sandwiches, a slice of rhubarb pie, and an extra candle. Not much. But not bad fare for a wounded bandito.

I had no intention of sticking around any longer than I had to tonight But I had a question or two on my mind that I wanted answered.

"How did you find these caves?" I asked. "And how do you know your men will come for you?"

Manuel grinned. "Are you worried about me, Harvey?"

I shook my head. "I just wanted to know."

"Well, gringo," he laughed, "it's none of your business. But since I know you will pester me, I'll tell you. To begin with," he said, chewing his long mustache, "soldiers are loyal. I am a good leader, and my men know this. They would rather have me than the chance of another who might be put in to replace me."

I nodded grudgingly. But that wasn't the only question I had. I took a chance—he seemed in good humor—so I pressed him a little further.

"Where is Pancho Villa right now?" I blurted. He laughed in my face, as though I were a child who had said something ridiculous—something I didn't understand.

"You are not the only one, Harvey, who asks where is Villa tonight!" He raised his eyes upward and moved his arm in a grand, sweeping motion. "The Redeemer is here, there, and everywhere. No one can stop him. He does not sleep—" He fixed his eyes on me. They seemed no longer dull and pain-ridden. There was a fire in them that reached out to touch me.

"He will not sleep until his people are liberated—until the oppressors of the people die!" The conviction in Manuel's voice sent a shudder through me.

"A brave jefe, this Pancho Villa," I cried. "Kills innocent men and preys on women. That is the way of a great redeemer—no?"

Manuel half-rose to his feet; I thought he would strike me. "Lies! Lies! They have fed you lies, gringo!"

I turned aside in disgust, but he reached out a hand to grab me—a claw that clamped around my wrist and drew me close. He didn't stop until his face was next to mine and his black eyes held me, as surely as his fingers against my flesh.

"Listen, I will show you what kind of a man is this Pancho Villa. I was with him—I saw with these very eyes. We stop in a village and meet there an old man. El viejo tells Villa that he is too old to work now. He will lose his ranch, his home. There are tears in his eyes. Pancho asks him—what does he owe? Two thousand pesos—two thousand pesos the old man tells him. Then he turns sadly away."

Manuel smiled to himself, remembering. His voice dropped to almost a reverent tone. "Pancho— he takes from his own pocket the money. He calls el viejo back to him. 'Take this dinero,' he cries, 'save your ranch, my brother!'"

There were tears in Manuel's eyes. He bent closer. "Always, always it is so with Villa. He gives food and money to the poor. He loves them. *What my country needs,* the people cry, *is Pancho Villa!*"

The last words Manuel spoke were a chant in praise of Villa. I had heard it before, but never the way Manuel said it.

"So, you are not a Maderista, but a Villista?" I asked.

"The Villistas fight for Madero," Manuel replied. "But our hearts belong to Villa."

I moved to pull away, but Manuel's fingers still held me. "Another thing," Manuel breathed, "you are only a child. You know nothing of men and wars and killing. Villa kills where he has to kill, and no more. *¿Comprendes?*"

I made no reply and Manuel continued. "You are stubborn, Harvey—for a gringo, you are. Listen, here is a story of Villa's killing. He ordered a man at a gringo mine to be shot. But first he commanded the man to remove his fine suit of clothing to give to a soldier. The man became angry and threw the coat in Villa's face." Manuel grinned, and his black eyes snapped in the yellow light of the candle. "This was courage—Pancho could admire a man like that. He set the man free. You see—there is Villa's great heart!"

He drew his hand away from my wrist with a flourish. "You are a child, and you are a gringo, but can you not see?"

I stood up. "I see that you love him, Manuel. I see that he is a great man to you. But you are right, I do not understand killing—for any reason, for any cause."

"Go away, Harvey," Manuel said in disgust, pulling at his mustache. "I am tired of you. But Harvey—tomorrow or the next day my men come. I can feel it. Then we will join our jefe again, we will fight beside him. We will cleanse our beloved country and make her free!"

I shivered and turned to go. "Gringo boy!" Manuel called out. He could make his voice mean and ugly. He did that now. "See that you are careful. I grow impatient holed up in this cave. My fingers are itching, my knife—she is honed to a fine sharp edge. I am hungry for fighting—do not bring me trouble. I am ready for any trouble you bring."

I nodded. "Mañana, Manuel."

He grinned. "Mañana! The moon rides high and full in the sky. My compañeros are riding. Mañana they will come for me."

Good riddance, I said to myself. *Good riddance. I won't be sorry to be rid of the likes of you! I can have my own life back again.*

I walked out of the cave mouth and onto the mountain. *My own life!* What was my life, anyway? What had it been before the Battle of Juarez and the night we played *Run, Sheep, Run?* It seemed too simple and too far away to remember. There was a boy who played and worked and went to school and argued with his sister. But that boy of a week ago wasn't me. I had changed, and more than Manuel had changed me.

The clock of the future was wound too tight. If the spring should break, there would be no safe, peaceful Mormon colony to run back to, no pattern I could fit into, no way to make all the pieces match as they used to. I could not hold the future in my hand as I could the past. The future was running by itself in a new direction, and like the strong spring current of the river, it swept me along.

Chapter Eleven

My mother had *not* died—not this time; a crisis had been averted by her patience and the doctor's care. She was spared to us for a little while yet, to see my father through hard times. I was grateful for that. But there was little else I was grateful for that next morning. The talk at school had taken a slight turn in direction.

"My dad owns land still back in the states." This from Wesley, of course. "We'd be rich if we moved back to Utah. I don't think I'd mind that."

Insufferable!

"I don't think it would make much difference, Wes, not for you," I couldn't help adding, though this was the first time I'd spoken to him since the day of the fight. "I still don't think you could get girls like Anna to dance with you!"

Everyone roared, and Wesley glowered. He wasn't certain how I came to know of his rejection.

"My dad says the schools in Utah are no better than our schools here," Willie bragged, turning the subject. I wondered if this could really be true. We in the colonies were proud of our schools. Dr. Maeser, superintendent of the entire Church school system, had come down to incorporate us as part of the organization. Even he had been impressed with what he saw.

The Academy building where we studied was only six years old, although there were four buildings in all. With a staff of eighteen teachers, we had some fine educational minds here. Graduation diplomas were offered in four departments—as well as certificates in music, domestic science and missionary training. We had a carpentry shop and a domestic arts department that boasted four new sewing machines. We also had a library and museum of our own and a school-sponsored band and orchestra whose members wore green uniforms trimmed in white braiding.

As I thought about it a deep pride welled up inside me. Even I had been part of the growth and the building of Juarez. I didn't want to go back to Utah rag-tag with my head hung between my shoulders. It disturbed me to think of a thing like that.

When I arrived home after school Alicia met me. "You're late," she said. "Father's looking for you."

My stomach did a flip-flop, but I answered her calmly, "Where is he?"

"Out in the barn," she answered. I turned to go, but she tugged at my shirt. "Here, Harvey. You can eat these as you go." She thrust into my hand a napkin holding a dozen cookies, warm yet from the oven. She smiled and floated along beside me, keeping pace.

"Anna missed you last night," she said in a carefully-cultivated voice of casual interest. "Where did you go, Harvey?"

"It's—"

"None of my business, I know," she hurried, beating me to it. "Aunt Clair said you were coming home to go to bed, but you didn't. When I got home, I looked in your room and you weren't there." A tight feeling was beginning to gnaw at the pit of my stomach. It was suddenly hard to swallow the mouthful of cookie I was chewing.

"You've turned into some sort of a detective, Alicia?" I blustered. "You ask questions about me, you search my room, you—"

"I did neither," Alicia defended herself. "Aunt Clair volunteered the information, and I only looked into your room, I didn't search it."

We were approaching the barn. If I could stall her with insults a few minutes longer, I might not have to come up with a real answer.

"I wouldn't say anything at all, Harvey," Alicia protested earnestly, "except that when Father came back last night, you weren't home yet. He wanted to know where you were—he was tired and angry a little, you know. So I—" She paused, looking very uncomfortable.

"What, Alicia? Did you lie to Father?" I couldn't believe it. Alicia lie! And for me! There was no sense to it.

"It wasn't a real lie," she replied defensively. "I merely told him I had seen you at the dance with your friends, and I was sure you'd be coming along in a little while." She ended, almost kindly, "That's all he needed to reassure him."

It was a lie of omission; Alicia was clever enough for that. She didn't mention the things she knew would disturb him, such as the fact that I'd disappeared mid-way through the dance. *If she had any idea where I had been!* I glanced over at her. What would Alicia think if she met Manuel? Seemed to me she could give him a run for his money.

"Thanks, Alicia," I said, not begrudgingly. "That was real decent of you—all things considered."

She threw me a smile that was a mixture of charm and mischief. "If Father happens to mention anything, I thought you should know."

I nodded. I reached for the leather cord that held the barn doors shut. "Harvey?" I turned. "Where *were* you?" The curiosity in Alicia's eyes was nearly blinding.

I sighed. "I'd like to tell you, I really would, but I can't Alicia. At least not yet."

"I'm your big sister—you can trust me! Haven't I proved that?" Her voice was raspy, half-shout, half-whisper.

"It's not that," I protested. "It's nothing I can explain. Oh, Alicia!" Something in my voice stopped her.

"All right, I'll give you a little time," she conceded. "But you'd better come up with some explanations soon."

"You're threatening me, Alicia," I said. "Don't do that."

"I'm not," she retorted. "Other people have eyes. Almonzo's worried about you. He said so!"

"Almonzo! How could *you* know?" That one threw me.

She smiled sweetly, her eyes veiled and far away. "There's so little you understand, Harvey," she murmured. "Poor boy."

With that she turned on her heel and left me. I felt like a young calf that had just been hog tied. Why was it Alicia always left me feeling that way?

Father didn't ask about last night. He had other things on his mind. One of his prize cows was ready to give birth and, as is often the case, there were complications.

"I want you to stay out here with Rafael, Harvey," he instructed, "and watch her. Send for me as soon as I'm needed." He looked haggard again, worried about the mouth and the eyes. "Your mother has a fever today, and she's restless. I'd like to be with her."

I hadn't even stepped into the house—I didn't know.

He laid his hand on my shoulder. "Don't worry, Harvey."

"How can you say that? You're worried to death yourself," I cried.

A strange expression came into his eyes and a slight smile warmed them. "I haven't paid much attention to you lately, Harvey. But that gives you no excuse to grow up on me overnight."

I didn't feel grown up. I felt small and lonely and tired. I didn't want to sit in the chilly barn all night. But his words seeped into me like a hot liquid, warming deeply.

"I'll be all right, sir," I said.

"Good," he answered. "Then so will I."

It was a strange thing for a father to say, especially my father. We spoke little together, he and I. He was usually gone, or when at the house, preoccupied. Only my mother could make his face awaken, only she could clear his mind so that his attention was hers alone. It was quite a power. I know Aunt Cleo envied it. I had envied it myself. Tonight, however, something different had happened between us. Not in words. But for that brief moment we said more to each other than we had all the rest of our lives.

The cow did not cooperate in the least. Helena brought my supper out to me. Rafael completed his chores, then curled up in a corner to whittle. The cow took her precious time, and I fumed. Rafael was a sullen type, no great company. He was a handsome young Mexican. All the señoritas were drawn to him, but he walked with a limp from an old childhood disease, and the limp made him mean and surly. When anyone got too close, he scared them away. My father hired him, out of compassion, I figured. I personally didn't like him about the place. But, of course, I had no say in such matters.

It was way past my bedtime when Father stepped into the barn.

"Nothing yet?" I held out my hands and shrugged my shoulders. He shook his head. "You'd best go to bed, then." He was tired himself. It was easy to see that. "Stop in and say goodnight to your mother," he reminded me.

"Of course," I said, feeling guilty at my intense relief to escape the barn and go to the house.

I was still in my mother's room, holding her thin white hand in mine when Helena came bustling in. "Your father needs you. The calf is coming."

I felt a great wave of anger, hot and hopeless, surge through my system. I had planned to go directly to my room, stay a few moments, then slip out to the cave. It was late already. I didn't want Manuel to get fidgety, and I didn't want to be out too late in the lonely darkness. We worked with the cow—Father, Rafael and myself—what seemed like all night and was in reality nearly three hours. The calf was in the wrong position, his nose tucked downward instead of thrusting forward and out, and his long legs coiled too far under his body. There's no way in the world you can rush a cow. First the calf's jaw, with Father's help, eased itself over his mother's pelvis. Then we waited for the feet to appear and the soft wet nostrils. A calf is such an angled, awkwardly-made sort of creature. No one was more relieved than I when we had him safely out, sniffing and taking a look at his new surroundings.

When at last Father gave me the word, I staggered back to the house and my bed. I had given up on Manuel long ago. But once under the covers I tossed and turned on the edge of sleep. At last I struggled up and pulled on my trousers. A full moon filled the sky as Manuel had said. Perhaps I ought to make the trip to the cave after all. The night was a waste as it was. I finished dressing and walked quietly through the still house and out the side door.

A wind had risen while I was in bed, an impatient wind that worried the dust at my feet into swirls and eddies and sent the old tree branches into protesting moans. I don't like the hidden voices a high wind carries, nor the shadows that dance to the wind's wild call. I paused by the edge of the barn, half-hesitating. A shadow trembled, then adjusted itself into a shape. The shape walked toward me. I stepped back with a cry.

"What you doing out of bed, Harvey? The calf, she is fine now." It was Rafael I had surprised. He grinned at me, but the grin was narrow and resembled a leer. "Or do you have something else on your mind, Harvey?"

I looked as disdainful as I could, though I was trembling. It struck me suddenly what Rafael himself might be about. I wondered if someone was in the barn with him right now.

"I believe it is you who has something on your mind," I said. I turned and walked back to the house. I could feel his eyes watching me, boring holes into my back. He was no friend of mine, I knew. But surely it stopped there. I had no reason to think he would personally harm me.

Nevertheless, the encounter increased the anxiety in my mind. I crawled back into bed, but my mind would not stop churning. When at last sleep came, it was troubled and uneasy and did little to rest me. I swam through one miserable dream after another.

At first Manuel's face leered at me, mean and narrow. Then he started laughing—he laughed 'til the sound pounded through my head. Then it was no longer Manuel, but Wesley laughing—two, three, then a dozen Wesleys laughing at me. Here the dream changed, and I was crawling up the mountain on my hands and knees. My pants legs were ripped and torn, and my hands were bleeding. Every time I reached out to secure a handhold there would be Manuel's knife—winking wickedly in a sun that blinded my eyes and sent a pounding noise through my head. No matter where my hand chose to go, the knife would be there before me, until at last it held me unmoving, a prisoner.

I woke up with the sensation of the knife point against my chest, and the palms of my hands feeling as though the skin had been sliced into ribbons. The roof of my mouth was dry; I could scarcely swallow. But I looked gratefully at my hands lying whole and untouched on the bedsheets. *Dreams—bad dreams, nothing more.* Relief flooded through me. There was nothing to worry about.

But that wasn't true. My mind, though exhausted still with the night's horrors, was yet clear enough to admit the truth: the worst part of last night's dream was a living nightmare. Manuel was real—and so was his fine-honed knife. Manuel had waited all night for a gringo boy who never came. What would the angry Villista do now?

Chapter Twelve

I went to school, but I couldn't concentrate on my studies. I kept thinking about Manuel lying in the dark cave waiting for me, rubbing his knife along his thumb and cursing all gringos. *Mexico for the Mexicans,* one of the revolutionary slogans boasted. *To hell with all gringos!*

"My fingers are itching," Manuel had said. "Do not bring me trouble." How much trouble did Manuel consider it? I asked myself over and over. How much trouble to wait all night and be disappointed?

I knew there was nothing for it. I'd have to go up there. I could take him my own lunch Helena had prepared. If I explained, at least he would know I hadn't deceived him. He might be angry, but at least he would no longer stalk the cave floor with some horrible picture in his mind of the Gringo boy bringing men with guns to meet him. I had not forgotten his threats of the first night: *If you betray me, Harvey, not only you will die,* he had promised, *but your padre and madre and the pretty gold-haired hermana. If you betray me. . .*

I made up my mind. When the lunch break came, I slipped out of the building, not saying a word to anyone, moving fast before Lewis could question me. I didn't think about what would happen when they discovered me missing. I would deal with that later. What mattered now was getting up the mountain to the cave and Manuel.

I cleared the school grounds with a sigh of relief.

Once away from the curiosity of my friends I should have no trouble. I reached the swinging bridge across the Piedras Verdes River, the "kissing bridge" that bisected Juarez. I had nearly crossed it when I heard a rattling sound under my feet, a noise that repeated itself in sharp rat-a-tats. I froze with my foot poised. Someone grabbed my ankle, and a voice called out "*Stop, runaway! I have a gun aimed at your head. Take one step, you're a dead man.*"

All sorts of horrible images raced through my mind. I expected Manuel or a dirty Villista to emerge from under the bridge, grim and angry. When it was Lewis' face that appeared, I could not believe it. I stared—and I'll give this much to him; he didn't laugh.

"Heck, Harvey, I didn't mean to really scare you." He shifted uncomfortably from foot to foot. "I was sure you'd seen me just when I ducked down under. I had to run like the dickens to beat you here."

I sat on the edge of the bridge. I hadn't spoken. He sat down beside me, swinging his legs. "Don't be sore at me, Harvey. It's not easy to fool you. I thought if nothing else, you'd recognize my voice." He chanced a cautious grin. "My accent was lousy. Did you really think a Villista had hold of you?"

I stood up. "I've got things to do, Lewis."

"That's fine." He smiled. "Where are we going? Lead on."

I faced him squarely. "You're not invited, Lew," I said. "This is my own business."

He shook his head. There was a mischievous gleam in his eye. "Sorry. You're not shaking me. Not this time, Harvey."

I started walking. He stuck to my heels like a well-trained dog. I stopped and turned on a sudden. We nearly collided. "I've got no time for your games," I said curtly. "Get lost, Lewis."

A stubborn look came over his face. "No, Harvey, you're comin' back to school with me, or I'm goin' with you."

"Who says so?" I threw back. I was growing angry—a trapped, up-against-the-wall kind of anger I didn't like.

"Me, for one." He stuck out his chin. "Isn't that enough, Harvey? Aren't we best friends?"

I couldn't relent! I shook my head. "That's why you can't come with me—that's why you should trust me!"

Poor Lewis was frustrated half out of his head. "It's *you* who doesn't trust *me*. Besides—" "He paused, gulping air. "Almonzo saw you!"

"Almonzo! He sent you. I should have known."

Lewis hung his head, a little ashamed for having told me.

"What did he say?" I demanded. Poor Lewis, he really squirmed.

"Almonzo said, 'All right, he's your best friend. Go get him, Lewis. Stick to him. If you lose him, you answer to me.'"

I felt deflated, as if someone had knocked the air out of me with one blow. There was nothing for it now but to go back, and I knew it.

"Come on, Lewis, if we run, we can make it before the bell rings."

Lewis didn't say another word—he was that

grateful. But I felt like the bull when the picadors and banderilleros close in. I knew this couldn't go on much longer. Once Almonzo got his teeth into something he didn't let go. Now there was Almonzo on one side and Manuel on the other. It was a pretty uncomfortable position for me!

We arrived just in time to slip into our seats before class started. Almonzo turned around and looked back at me, but I dropped my eyes. That would have been enough for anyone else but Almonzo. He rose and walked over to where I was sitting.

"I'd have gone for you myself if you hadn't come back." It was a firm, matter-of-fact statement.

"I know. Why do you think I'm here?" I still didn't look up to meet his eyes.

He set his hand briefly on my shoulder. "We'll talk later, Harvey." The teacher had entered the room. Almonzo went back to his seat.

I thought: *I have just 'til the end of school to come up with some answers!* I had no idea how wrong I was, nor under what circumstances I would next see Almonzo, nor how much would happen before that time.

Chapter Thirteen

Exactly fifty-three minutes before school was to be dismissed for the day, the door of our classroom flew open with such force that it banged against the wall and reverberated. In charged Johnny Allen, one of the oldest Academy students. I didn't know Johnny well, but anyone who saw him could tell he had suffered some kind of a shock. His eyes were three times their normal size and looked glazed with sheer horror. Small beads of perspiration had gathered along his upper lip and across his forehead. He was breathing in deep gasps and running his hand through his hair with fingers that trembled.

"Excuse me, ma'am, but the principal sent me," he blurted out. "There's a group of Maderistas tearin' through town. They've been shooting things up pretty bad."

He paused to gulp air; the classroom gulped with him. Mrs. Madsen, a sensible woman, replied evenly: "Do they have guns, Johnny? Has anyone been shot?"

"I don't rightly know, ma'am. Will Forsythe said he heard from the delivery boy at his father's store that they drew guns on two men in the street and threatened to string 'em up by—"

"That's enough, Johnny," Mrs. Madsen interrupted. "What are the principal's instructions?"

"You are to dismiss class, and the students hightail it home if they know what's good for them— those were his words, ma'am, zakly," he blurted, still not able to catch his breath.

"Thank you, Johnny." Though Mrs. Madsen stifled a smile, I thought she had grown a little pale. "There's nothing to *worry* about—" she began, lingering over the word "worry." But Johnny didn't allow her to finish her thought.

"Guns or no, they're mean, ma'am, and they're stealin' everything they can get their hands on!" She threw him a withering glance this time. "Gather up your books, boys and girls, in an orderly fashion. I think it would be wise to follow our leader's instructions."

We were not as quiet nor as orderly as Mrs. Madsen wished, but we got out of there in record time, you can believe it. There was much wild conjecture about the deeds that had been done—evil, exciting deeds right under our noses! The wild talk covered an uneasy layer of stark cold fear.

I walked as far as I could with Lewis, then headed straight home. I was deathly curious about one thing: *Were these Manuel's men?* I wasn't sure if I wished they were, or I'd rather they weren't. Had Manuel climbed down off the mountain? Did he ride with them?

I hadn't even reached the front porch when Helena came running, wringing her apron into knots. I could see she'd been crying.

"¡Gracias a Dios! Thank heavens, Harvey," she cried, "you are here!"

At first I thought something was wrong with Mother! My heart seemed to turn cold as a ball of ice and ache in my chest.

"Tu padre, he is not home. We have no one to turn to. You must—"

"For heaven's sake, Helena," I shouted, "what is it?"

She stared at me with round, fearful eyes. "Alicia!" The way she said the name sent a charge of fear running through me.

"What has happened to Alicia?" I nearly begged. "Please tell me, Helena."

"The Maderistas, they have been here," she blubbered. "They came in through there—" She pointed to the spot, "and rounded up tu padre's cattle and all of the horses."

"The horses should have been safe in the old south pasture," I shouted. "How is it they were right here, all nicely gathered for the Villistas?"

She gazed at me, not really comprehending. "Rafael had not taken them yet to the pasture."

He had his own reasons, I thought to myself. *I'll deal with him later.* Helena was staring at me. "Go on," I urged her.

She held out her hands in a helpless gesture. "Alicia—she go after him."

"She went after who?" My mind was still churning.

"The Maderistas, they take the horse. She go after Starfire."

What an idiot! Why didn't I see that the first time? *They took all the horses!* I had been too engrossed with my own petty revenge.

"Where? Where?" I cried.

Again she pointed. "Down there, by the cottonwood grove. You must stop her, Harvey!"

I was already running. Her voice was lost in the

sound of my feet and my own rapid breathing. The grove didn't cover much ground, but it was dense and would be easy to hide in. My only hope was to reach Alicia before she found the stallion!

When I came to the first line of trees, I slowed down some. I listened as hard as I could and crept cautiously forward. The light in the grove was dim, and my footsteps muffled. I heard no sounds for a minute or two. Perhaps, I dared to hope, I was lucky! Perhaps there were no men in the grove—no stolen horses.

The laugh shattered that hopeless wish as it shattered the stillness. The tree branches seemed to tremble. I froze in place. The sound came from mere feet away. The Villistas were here, then! Was Starfire among them? Where was Alicia?

It took long minutes that seemed like hours for me to muster courage enough to edge forward. A dense pocket of trees filled a slight dip ahead. The muffled voices came from in there. I drew closer. It seemed every step I took sounded as loud as a gunshot now. I sought for a large wide tree, and when I found one, I gratefully plastered myself against it. My breathing hurt in my chest. I felt any moment a hairy hand would reach round the tree and grab me.

At last I adjusted my position and moved my head slowly until I could see into the thicket. There was a good-sized cluster of horses, many of which carried my father's brand. And Starfire, tall and white, stood like a prince among them.

I counted five men: one lay stretched out on the ground, one sat squat on a tree stump, two had their backs to me, working over the horses. The last, tall and lean-looking, paced impatiently back and forth across the small clearing. They all resembled Manuel. They were dirty and unkempt, their hair matted, their faces unshaven. One wore a worn gray patch over his left eye. The man who paced had a pistol stuck into his belt. They had guns! My eyes scanned up and down, looking carefully now for other weapons. The scuffed boots might conceal long sharp knives like Manuel's. I hesitated. I saw no way to get Starfire and the other animals out of their hands.

For a moment I had forgotten my errand—forgotten Alicia. That one moment was enough. I saw a flash of white, and a flash of gold. In a blur they moved forward. I rubbed my hand across my eyes. *Alicia!*

She moved noiselessly through the trees like some kind of wood sprite. No leaves crunched under her swift, light foot. Her long hair, like a mantle, flowed behind her as she flowed with equal and effortless grace through the men in the clearing.

She was mere paces away from her horse when the leader spied her. He grunted in surprise, then glanced swiftly around in all directions, his keen eyes searching for the other intruders who must be there. Alicia never paused. The man nearest to her grabbed for her arm and grazed her slender ankle as her foot swung up and over Starfire's body.

She sat tall on his back, her fingers wound into his mane and her head thrown high in breathless triumph. In that one frozen instant she knew she had won. Her blue eyes glowed, reflecting some inner fire.

"This is my horse!" she cried. Her voice snapped sharp through the still clearing, like the cracking of brittle tree limbs in the wild spring current. "He was not meant to carry a Maderista. You had no right to take him."

Starfire danced forward. He was catching some of her high excitement. The men stirred. The lean man's hand moved to cover his pistol. *Cut out the theatrics, Alicia!* I silently pleaded. *For heaven's sake, get the heck out of here!*

She seemed to hear. She tossed her gold head. She bent low in the saddle. The lean man swore and muttered something under his breath. As if on signal he and his men moved forward. The man with the patch jumped bareback onto his horse and urged it forward. It was useless. They were clumsy, wooden figures beside the stallion who gathered his magnificent strength beneath him and swept through the clearing with the grace of a fawn.

In one leap he cleared the stump and the startled man who had half-left his seat there. The man stumbled backward a step or two, watching the spot where the girl and the horse had been: the woods closed around it, the leaves trembled slightly, then all was still.

The lean man swore again as he mounted his own horse and rode after his friend. I knew their chase would be fruitless. Alicia and Starfire had a head start, and none of these mounts would be able to touch them. Besides, she knew the terrain. I pushed back the thick branches. The stallion was soaring along the ground; it was pleasure to watch him. The distance between Starfire and his pursuers widened with each sweeping stride.

I thought I knew what Alicia would do. Where the ground took a harsh dip a few yards ahead she would dart into the narrow dry creek bed and double back here, protected by the thick growth along the old waterway. I couldn't see to be sure, but a few minutes later the two hombres reappeared, pushing their mounts, looking very angry. The tall man pulled his horse up short and leapt out of the saddle. He was breathing heavily, and his eyes looked narrow and mean.

He laughed and, as if on cue, the others laughed with him. "We will get back the big white one," he boasted. "And anything else we want here." He scanned the woods once more with a searching gaze. His eyes seemed to find mine through the cover of leaves and lock upon them with a hot and desperate intensity. Suddenly he swirled around. "¡Vámonos!" he commanded curtly. "Let's get out of here."

Of course they would no longer consider the grove a safe spot for even temporary cover. They herded the animals and moved in a tight group through the trees, heading toward the low mountains. I waited a few more minutes, then turned around and walked home alone through the angry silence.

I walked straight to the barn. As I had thought, I found Alicia there with Starfire. "He's not safe here," I told her curtly. She looked up with wide eyes that still reflected the wonder and fear of her wild adventure.

"I told Rafael to watch him. I'll spend as much time with him myself as I can."

I snorted. There was more bitterness in my voice than I expected. "It will do you no good to rely on Rafael. He can't be trusted."

She drew in her breath and her bright eyes clouded. "What do you mean?" It was Alicia's usual demand, but softly spoken.

I sighed audibly. "Rafael let them in here, Alicia. And he had the horses conveniently ready and waiting, not safe in the south pasture as he had been instructed."

She gave a slight nod. "Father will be angry, I'm afraid. His prize mare is missing, and all of Mother's goats, and a good number of cattle."

I caught a sudden movement at the end of the barn. "Rafael!" I shouted. "I know you're back there. Show yourself, you worthless coward!"

He walked slowly out from the shadows. His face was dark with insolence and bravado. My fingers clenched into a fist that itched to plant itself into that face!

"You make accusations like a spoiled child, Harvey," he said and shrugged his thin shoulders. "I have done nothing wrong. You can prove nothing."

"We'll see," I retorted. "Meanwhile, I can do one thing. I can throw you off this place, and that's just what I'm doing. You'd better be long gone before my father gets here!"

The threat sounded petty and childish, and that annoyed me. Rafael's eyes smouldered, but he merely shrugged again. "It's nothing to me," he replied. "I have more important things to do now."

I felt new anger surge through my veins. "That

sounds grand, Rafael, very grand and important. You mean to join up with the Villistas?"

He smiled a thin, condescending smile and began to turn from me.

"Where are these mighty warriors, these Villistas?" I cried.

"I shall find them," he boasted. "I have ways."

"You have nothing," I scoffed. "Try the caves. In the caves you will find what you look for. That is, if you're man enough to go there."

He didn't answer. He kept on walking. Alicia put her hand on my arm, but I pulled away from her roughly. I began moving. I had made up my mind on my walk from the grove.

"Harvey, stop this moment! Where are you going?"

"I'm going to have this thing out with Manuel once and for all," I told her. Her face showed dismay and confusion. "Tell Helena not to wait dinner for me."

I took a few steps, then turned back around to face her. It was only fair, and I couldn't help myself, anyway.

"You were magnificent, Alicia. I've never seen anything like you and Starfire in my life."

She looked down at her feet. "You were there?" Her voice was a whisper. When she turned her face up again, her eyes were glistening.

"Helena sent me to save you," I explained, not able to suppress a short, derisive laugh. "I should have known that wouldn't be necessary."

I tried to smile, but I don't think I was very

successful. I continued walking. In a moment Alicia, recovered, called after me.

"Where *are* you going, Harvey? And who is Manuel?"

I didn't answer. I kept a firm, steady pace. The anger was strong still. It was like a power that overcame all fear, all doubt, all pain. I couldn't wait to reach the caves, and Manuel.

Chapter Fourteen

I took a circuitous route to the caves, purposefully bypassing any homes or ranches where I might be recognized, or questioned. I did not see the men from the grove nor any others, but at times I saw evidence of their passing: a busted gate hanging on one hinge, a whole line of ocotillo fence broken down and trampled to pieces, a lone cow wandering far off from fields or fence line. At one ranch I saw goods scattered in the yard—dishes, corn meal, potatoes. I wondered if someone at that ranch had defied and angered the tall, lean Villista.

I reached the path leading up to the caves. It looked silent, deserted, unchanged from two days before. Had the revolutionaries used it? I saw no footprints, no telltale signs of their passing. Perhaps these were not Manuel's men. Perhaps they knew nothing of him or the caves. I began climbing.

I had somehow expected to find Manuel stretched out on his blankets, quiet and waiting, as he had been the times before. Or at least that was the picture I carried in my head, without thinking. I was never a great one to think things through—my being here showed that. As I approached the mouth of the cave I heard muffled voices. There was a dim light gleaming inside. Manuel had lit candles. He was not alone. Were the men from the grove with him?

I took one step across the threshold of the cave and hard steel stopped me—a long rifle barrel was thrust against my chest.

"¿Qué pasa?" a cold voice called. "Who goes there?"

I pushed the barrel aside and answered in Spanish. "I have my own business with your jefe, soldier—not with you." I hardly took time to look at the man I spoke to. My eyes were searching for Manuel. There were three men standing in a close knot together, conversing, their backs to me. I didn't recognize any of them. One turned around slowly. His eyes fell on me. No smile lit them. He raised the bottle he held to his lips and took a long drink, then threw back his head and snorted, *"This* is medicine, gringo boy, sí? You should try some. Good for what ails you, Harvey, is that not so?" He spoke in Spanish, and his men watched him, their mouths open in surprise, their eyes wary.

"You look the grand leader now," I said, with a sweeping motion. And he did. He had wound a wide silk cloth of many colors around his middle. It tied in a fringed knot at one side and succeeded in hiding most of the dingy, stained bandage. A tall new sombrero was perched at a cocky angle on his head, and the boots he wore looked new also.

"You act the grand leader, too," I added, "drinking and boasting." His dark brow knit. He swaggered over to stand beside me, the bottle he clutched in his left hand swinging drunkenly.

"You no come to feed Manuel, but you come to insult him—sí, my little gringo game cock?" He laughed, but his eyes were dark and brooding.

"You have a short memory, Manuel," I retorted, my voice hard and angry. "I bring food, blankets, candles, medicine—I keep you alive. *And* I keep my mouth shut!" I ended emphatically.

"Last night! What about last night, Harvey?"

"I didn't come last night—"

"I know, I know!" He rubbed his belly and patted it hard. His watching men snickered and laughed, but Manuel ignored them. "I worked with my father all night in the barn delivering a calf."

Manuel snorted. "A likely story! You go soft on me, my little gringo. You crawl into your safe warm bed and forget Manuel." The men laughed again, but I scarcely heard them.

"I should have brought my father, then, would you have preferred that? I should have told him I had a date with a Villista in a miserable cave on the mountain. Or perhaps I should have brought the surly peon boy who stopped me when I went out later—the same peon who fancies himself a friend of the revolutionaries and who opened my father's gates to your men!"

I realized I was shouting. Manuel took a step backward and folded his arms across his chest. "I risked my life and kept my word," I persisted, "and what does it teach me?"

Manuel thrust his head forward and growled deep in his throat. It was like a challenge. Something inside impelled me to take it. "A man keeps his word—and a Villista repays him with treachery!"

In the silence that followed my words I could hear my own breathing. It sounded as painful as it felt. All eyes were upon me—black eyes that snapped

and smouldered. The anger was seeping out of me,
leaving a weariness in its place. I don't know what
Manuel had in his mind to do; I will never know that.
For suddenly the cave mouth filled with a chaos of
shouts and laughter.

I turned and saw the men from the grove stamping in among us. The tall, lean one rudely pushed
some of his comrades aside as he worked his way
forward. He didn't stop until he stood in front of
Manuel.

"*Mi jefe*—my chief," he said, with respect in his
tone. "At the foot of these hills in a little canyon we
have gathered supplies to take back to Villa!"

Wild shouts of praise and approval interrupted his
boast. His thin mouth parted in a taut grin of
acknowledgement, but his eyes remained on the
watching face of Manuel.

"Sheep and cattle and flour," he continued. "Fast
horses—and Mormon guns!" Another shout went up.
"We shall ride back to Villa in triumph, compañeros!"

I, too, watched Manuel's face. I could not read it.
I stepped closer to him and spoke into his ear, in
Spanish. "Your men steal from the kind, the good, the
law-abiding. That is woman's work! Would that
please your Redeemer?"

"Shut up, Harvey," Manuel snapped. "You are
like a bothersome gnat buzzing in my ear. I've a mind
to swat you."

"The Mormons are your friends," I reminded him.
But he turned at me wildly.

"If they are our friends, then they will serve us as

friends do, sí? We must have food and horses and
guns to fight. Even Mormon gringos know that. We
can't destroy our enemies with wishes and good
intentions."

"Who is this puny gringo who insults us in our
own tongue?" the tall Villista demanded. Manuel hesitated, and the lean man misunderstood his hesitation.
With one thrust of his arm he swept me back. I lost
my footing and stumbled. One of the Villistas
reached out and caught me by one elbow, or I would
have fallen.

Still Manuel's face remained closed, almost void
of expression. But he reached out with a clawlike
hand and closed his grip around the neck of the man
beside him.

"Harvey is the son of a great Mormon jefe, and he
is my friend. You shame me in front of my friend!"
he shouted. The lean man's eyes, that could be so
cruel, were filled now with terror.

"Who picked you out of the gutter and fed you?"
Manuel spat.

"Yourself," the man answered.

"Who taught you to ride and shoot and made you
a soldier—a mighty Villista?" Manuel snarled.

"Yourself," the man repeated.

Manuel tightened his grip on the lean man's neck.
He was near to choking now, but he made no struggle. "You are a proud peacock, Juan. You do not
remember your place and be grateful."

I could see why Manuel was a lieutenant. María's
adoration might not be as misplaced as I once had
thought it. He released Juan, then turned his back
upon him. Juan showed no protest.

Manuel strode over to where I stood. I could
swear, I could almost swear he winked at me! When
he spoke, some of the harshness had gone from his
voice.

"I apologize for Juan's rudeness. You were right,
Harvey; you have been my friend. Now I shall be
yours." He looked around, then said something swiftly under his breath to one of his men. "A meal is
ready. Will you stay and eat with a wild bunch of
Villistas, gringo?"

My heart banged against my chest. I was surprised at how eagerly I accepted Manuel's invitation.
"It will be a pleasure," I replied.

"Well, at least an adventure, Harvey," Manuel
chuckled.

There was a sudden commotion at the cave's
entrance. I drew in my breath. The hombre who
entered, disheveled and wild-eyed with fear and
pride, was that little devil, Rafael!

One of the men shoved him forward. "We have a
new recruit, a volunteer, jefe." His voice held a tinge
of mockery in it. Rafael threw his head back and
approached Manuel with the cockiness peculiar to
young Mexican men.

Perhaps he was thinking: *I'll show that miserable,
overbearing Harvey. See—I am here—and the chief
himself wants to see me!* He may have thought something like that, for when his gaze fell upon me, standing beside Manuel, his eyes grew sick and frightened,
and a low moan escaped his lips.

Manuel did not miss this. "What ails you, hombre? Come forward. We will not bite your head off."

He laughed, but Rafael's features did not brighten. He threw a panicked glance at me, and Manuel caught it. "What—are you afraid of the small pale gringo?"

It was my turn to laugh. "Sí, Manuel, and well he should be."

Manuel grunted and knit his dark brow. "What is this?" he demanded.

Rafael seemed to shrink. I half-expected him to turn and run, but he held his ground.

"This boy—" and I used the word purposefully, rather than man. "This boy—he is no good to you. He has acted the traitor to the kind man who took him in when he was homeless and friendless. This man fed him, clothed him, gave him work, paid him well—" I paused. "And trusted him. He betrayed his friend—he would betray you also."

Manuel chewed on the end of his mustache and said nothing. He had been sizing up Rafael as I spoke. Rafael squirmed beneath his gaze.

"Does the gringo speak true, boy?" His voice was low, but it carried a deep sense of authority. Rafael took this to be his chance. His lips parted over his teeth in a kind of sneer. "The gringo is loco. I know nothing of this treachery he speaks of. I serve no master. I serve the revolution!"

"The revolution," Manuel spoke slowly, "is a very hard master. Much harder than Señor Hales, muchacho."

"I want to serve my country and kill the oppressors!" Rafael cried.

Manuel slowly shook his head. "I don't think so. I

think you will first serve yourself, and second the revolution." He ran his hand across the silk cloth that covered his bandaged wound. "There is little of glory in war, my friend. But there is much of pain and fear and hunger."

He shook his head; this time more emphatically. "We have no use for this man." He turned to me. "Do you want him, Harvey?"

For a moment I was confused. Why ask such a question? Of course I did not want Rafael. Surely he could find somewhere else to go, some other work. Then it hit me. The revolutionaries, I had heard, try a man against their standards and if he falls short, if he fails, if he proves a hazard—they dispose of him very dispassionately.

Manuel saw the realization pass over my face like a dark shadow. He did not smile nor lighten my discomfort. "Sí, Harvey. A bullet is swift and painless. We rid the world of a little more trouble." He shrugged. "Do we take care of this coward, or do you want him?"

I took a few steps forward until I stood facing Rafael.

"You heard el jefe." Rafael's face was leaden, and he dropped his eyes to avoid mine. "Do I give you to the Villistas as you would have given us to them?"

The enmity in my own voice surprised me. So did the pleading look in Rafael's eyes.

"I am not the man my father is," I told him. "But I am his son. I know what he expects of me." I took a deep breath. "Go home, Rafael. Go home to my father. Tell him what you've done. He'll deal justly with you."

"I will go!" Rafael cried. "Gracias, Harvey." He didn't wait for Manuel to change his mind. He ran through the black mouth of the cave and was swallowed by darkness.

"Well, I am hungry," Manuel said, grinning at me. I could read satisfaction in his eyes. "Can we eat now, do you think, Harvey?"

I nodded. "Sí, jefe," I said, "that sounds good to me."

The men cleared space on the cave floor where serapes were spread for us to sit on. I saw now in a corner a large pot filled with some kind of stew boiling over a low fire. I wondered which of my neighbor's chickens we would be eating, but I said nothing. I sat cross-legged beside Manuel. A man handed us each a tin plate piled high with rice, chicken, beans and fresh flour tortillas.

I was surprised at how good it all tasted. There was nothing to wash it down with but bottles of liquor. Manuel sent a man out for a canteen from one of the horses so that I might have water.

The men warmed and relaxed under the influence of food and drink in their bellies. Some began boasting of brave deeds they had done, or those they would do in the future. Suddenly the short, stocky man who had been squatting on the tree stump when Alicia and Starfire jumped over remembered that he, too, had a tale to tell. In rapid staccato Spanish he told it, describing the milk-white horse and the golden-haired girl.

The men roared with laughter and slapped their thighs, but Juan darkened and grew noticeably surly, especially when the men began mocking him for being made the fool by a pretty gringa girl. He spat into the dirt.

"The gringa girl will be sorry," he boasted. "I will yet ride her fancy horse myself, and teach her a lesson!"

Some scoffed, but others encouraged his boasting. I thought it was time to add my two cents' worth. I stood.

"The gringa girl," I announced, "is my sister. The white horse was a gift from a Spanish gentleman when she was a little girl. She values it above her own life. I think you know that."

There were vague mumblings from the men. Juan muttered something ugly under his breath, but I didn't quite catch it.

"You have many of my father's most valuable animals," I continued. "You have no right to take what doesn't belong to you—what others have worked hard for—no matter what your cause!" I saw Manuel roll his eyes and cross himself quickly.

"Shut him up," one of the men called out.

"All right," I cried, "you have taken what you feel justified in taking. But you are not as smart as your leader, Pancho Villa. Doesn't Villa admire spirit and courage? Villa would give the gringa señorita her horse because of her bravery, and he would want you to do the same. It would be bad luck to do anything different. Sí, Manuel?"

For a moment there was silence, then Manuel threw back his great head in a roar of laughter. "Sí, Harvey. I have taught you well! Sí, Harvey."

I smiled back at Manuel. I couldn't help it. I felt relieved for the first time since I'd entered the cave. Perhaps now would be a good moment to make my exit. "I must go home," I told Manuel. "My father will worry."

He nodded and I started walking the length of the cave, but a sharp voice stopped me.

"You let the boy go to bring back Mormon men with guns?" the voice asked, and half a dozen others took up the question. Manuel didn't move from the place he stood. He shrugged his shoulders.

"You are a bunch of old women," he scoffed. "Harvey can be trusted. He will not bring back men for our rifles to pick off one by one. Fools!" He lifted his voice a little. "The Mormons know we are here. They don't need Harvey to tell them."

I began walking again. "That's right," I heard another man say. "The Mormons don't scare too easy, but they don't want trouble. This is a fine, safe place to set up operations. I say we make this a base and work the countryside round about here."

I stopped in my tracks. His words stopped me. Could he be serious? The voices I heard were all loud in agreement. A sudden realization of what that would mean flooded over my senses.

We would be forced to abandon Colonia Juarez as my father and the other men had predicted. We would go back as beggars to the Great Salt Lake and Mount Timpanogos. Our homes, our stores, the Academy, all would be silent. Or overrun by an army of peons.

The talk continued, like the buzzing of angry bees just inside my head. These filthy, pathetic wretches

were talking calmly of our destruction! I had one
wild and terrible chance, but I had to take it. A crazy,
cock-eyed scheme—but the only hope I could see. I
couldn't believe I was going to do it—I with my
"healthy respect" for the dead and my cowardly fears.
I turned around slowly and lifted my voice above the
hubbub.

"This is Mexico, your country—not gringo country," I said. The men stared at me. I was stating the
obvious. It annoyed them. I went on. "But long
before your people, a great nation of white men lived
here." Their annoyance grew. Several made scoffing
sounds.

"Get rid of this gringo idiot!" one of them shouted.

"Why do you think the Mormons prosper here?" I
persisted. "They work hard. They are honest citizens,
yes. They are also protected by the white goddess of
the mountains." The men stared at me, trying to size
up my preposterous statement.

"It is true," I said, retracing my steps to the center
of the cave where a candle in a crude wooden holder
sat burning. I picked it up, and the motion threw
shadows along the cave wall, shadows that stretched
and disappeared into pockets of inky black darkness.

"The lady of the mountain favors these people of
her own color. It pleases her when they prosper and
are happy. With her great powers she will bless those
who help them—" I paused and directed my gaze
upon Juan where he stood watching me darkly. "And
curse any who may set his hand against them."

I saw one Villista cross himself hurriedly. Juan

growled and took a step forward. Even Manuel
looked angry.

"Harvey, what is this nonsense? We want no nonsense from you! Go home where you belong."

"Come see for yourselves!" I threw the words out
like a challenge. A cold shudder ran over my frame. I
don't know about the Villistas, but I had scared
myself half to death. There was nothing more horrify-
ing to me than the thought of the lady sitting in her
cold chamber, waiting with sightless eyes for our
approaching.

There was little response. Clutching the candle
firmly I walked as far as I dared toward the back
recesses of the cave. Standing in my little puddle of
light I repeated the challenge.

"Who is coming? Are you all cowards? Who will
pay homage to the gringa goddess in her cave?"

They moved singly at first, then in comfortable
clumps of twos and threes. Several carried candles or
torches. I was happy to see that. There were fourteen
men counting Manuel. I made fifteen. I hoped we
could all fit inside the lady's small chamber. "Follow
me, " I said, "and be silent. If you show her proper
respect, you may gain her favor."

There is a long network of caves, linked one to
another, feeding how deep into the heart of the mountain no one knows. Like a sprawling serpent the
caves wind back, but they are deceptive. There are
arms of the serpent that lead off here and there to
break the winding pattern. Some of these end in useless dead ends—others, they say, go on without end-
ing. Still others break off abruptly, cut short by deep

holes and abysses. If a man falls into one of these, he is never found. I thought grimly: *Those black holes could easily swallow a small gringo boy and a dozen Villistas.*

It had been months since my friends and I had ventured back into the caves. Could I find my way there? Could I locate the lady's chamber? With each step my confidence drained from me. I hadn't thought of the consequences to myself if I didn't find her! We entered one compartment, then through a narrow neck passed into another. The men behind me were growing restive. By my calculations there should be one more wide, sprawling cavern and near its exit three paths to choose from: The right was the main path, the middle a dud, the left led to the lady's chamber.

I was right, but how massive the bulbous cave was! When at last we neared the end, the three holes stared like frowning black eyes at us. There was a sudden murmur of expectation, and then a silence. Some of the men started down the main path, but I waved them back.

The narrow aisle to the left ended at the mouth of the lady's outer chamber. When we got there, I pushed back the large boulder that blocked the entrance. Manuel helped me. The rock scraped the cave's floor with a screech of disturbed protest. The men coughed and shifted their weight, and conversed in whispers. Several swore under their breaths, but I don't think it helped much.

I know there was nothing to lighten the fear that gripped at my own heart. I don't like to meddle with the dead; I don't think it's healthy. I never felt comfortable myself, gawking at the lady, like she was some kind of a carnival side show. The lady looked fierce, even in ancient death, and I always had wondered what kind of a person she'd been in life. Perhaps not sympathetic at all to young boys and their antics. Perhaps like Alicia, vain and flippant. Or perhaps like my mother, and it offended her even now to be pointed to and stared at. Anyhow, I hoped the gruesome Villistas would not be too much for her. I stooped and passed through the jagged hole, and the others followed.

The outer chamber was nothing unusual, except that a door, a real door, had been set in the far rock wall. On this side a worn but ornately-carved wooden handle had been attached to pull the door outward. The other side was smooth and unmarred, with no means provided to open the door once it was secured in place. Someone long ago had imprisoned the lady behind that door. Why she was held there, how long she had lived, what her dying thoughts were . . . those were secrets time guarded with jealous silence. But there were tales: old legends and new stories. May the lady forgive me for the embellishments I was about to add.

We clustered near the door, those holding candles pushing close. The streams of light fell along the smooth panels. I looked at Manuel. His eyes were wide dark pools, but I saw no fear in them. I thought suddenly of that other woman, his woman, María, whom I'd never seen. I addressed the men, but my gaze was fixed solidly on Manuel's calm features.

"Behind that door," I said, "sits the white goddess. Long ago her people lived here, waged war, built mighty cities, sacrificed to ancient gods, and prospered. The lady was once a great warrior-leader. In death her powers are strong. She commands many spirits."

I wrapped my fingers around the carved handle. "Enter into her presence with care. You are her guests here. You shelter in her caves. You hunt in her mountains. You forage the countryside that lies under her protection. Behold, the white goddess of Chihuahua."

I pulled hard. The wood panels groaned, the door inched open. With a long sigh the disturbed air churned; our candles wavered. I flung the door wide and raised my eyes in search of the lady.

It took a moment for my sight to focus. At first I saw nothing. Then the shadows and shades and impressions merged into definable shapes. The lady sat on her high ledge, an outcropping of rock that was smooth and hollowed out much like a chair, and set high in the tall cliff wall where no hands could reach her. The rock behind her, reflecting the candles' light, seemed to glow with a pulse of its own. The skin of the lady's face was parchment thin, stretched tight like old leather, but one could see that it had once been light, fair skin. And though her eyes were mere sockets and her mouth a narrow sunken slash, somehow you could tell that in life the lady had been beautiful. Wisps of long hair hung about her cheeks and draped over her shoulder—long yellow hair that had faded to look like dull spun gold. Her shrunken neck was hidden by layers of gold necklaces, sparkling with deep inset jewels and diamonds. These blinked at us now like small, furtive eyes that flared into life when the candle light caught them.

Her thin arms were covered halfway to the elbows with jeweled bracelets. Her gown had been sewn with many jewels, and the cloth she sat on had once been thick and fine and many-colored. All this one could half-see, half-sense. The regal aspect, the gaunt, startled, anguished look on the lady's features seemed to scream with the teeming emotions that had frozen with her death—but had not died!

My eyes went of their own accord in search of the point of dread, the point of mystery—the ancient blade buried to the hilt in the lady's ribs. A cry of startled fear sent shivers along my spine! Manuel crossed himself and stared at my face. *It had been my own cry!*

"*¿Qué es esto?*—What is it?" he whispered. I pointed. I could not speak yet.

All eyes froze on the point of the blade—the narrow, ivory-handled blade that the lady clutched in her bony, jeweled fingers! The thin, hard tip was pointed outward. It seemed to me if the lady lunged, if she thrust her arm forward, the knife would bury itself in my flesh.

At last my words came, hoarse and breathless. "The cruel blade the lady holds and points at our hearts," I said, and felt the men tremble—"that same blade when last I gazed on the lady, was sunk deep into her ribs!" I shuddered. "She brandishes it now—heaven help us!—I don't know why."

I turned. I had done all I had come here to do and

then some. The Villistas could linger for reasons of their own if they had a mind to. I wanted nothing more to do with the lady.

I clutched my candle tightly and startled walking. Each step I took put the lady and her glittering weapon behind me. I didn't need to turn around to know the Villistas followed, as silently and swiftly as I.

Chapter Fifteen

I thought of many things on my way back down the mountain. I knew I would never solve the mystery of the lady. There were other mysteries, and some were inside me, but I was too weary, too churned up to make sense of my thoughts and feelings.

Not until I approached the house did I think of my father. I had thought about him back in the cave when I confronted Rafael. Now it was not Rafael, but I who must face him.

The lights in the barn lured me to postpone the moment. I pushed through the door, my eyes blinking and narrowing as the light struck them.

Alicia saw me before I saw her and ran toward me. "Thank heaven you're home and safe!" she cried.

Someone moved in the shadows behind her. I thought it might be Rafael, but it was Almonzo. He walked closer until the light fell full upon him. Somehow he was the last person I'd expected to find here. I was about to question, to protest, and then I remembered the night of the dance and the way he had looked at Alicia.

"I asked Almonzo to help me protect Starfire," she said quickly, watching my face. I nodded. Almonzo was watching me, too.

"Where have you been?" he asked, knowing this time I would tell him.

"I have been to the caves."

"The Villistas are there?"

I nodded. Alicia bit her lip, but had sense enough to say nothing.

"You have known all along the Villistas were coming?"

"No!" I protested. "And yes, in a way." He waited for me. His eyes were bright with interest and warm with the kindness that is his nature.

"The night we played *Run, Sheep, Run* a wounded Villista caught me. He forced me to help him up to the cave where he could hide safely until his men came for him." Alicia gasped and covered her mouth. This was too much for her.

"You told no one? Not even your father?"

"That's right. I couldn't. He had a gun and a long wicked knife, and he knew who I was. He knew my father, and he knew of my golden-haired sister."

The muscles twitched in Almonzo's face and his black eyes blazed, but he said nothing.

"I wished a dozen times it had been someone else," I confessed. "You, Almonzo. You could have handled the whole thing much better than I."

"No, Harvey, that's not true," he replied in his quiet way. "What made you go back when you knew his men were with him?"

"I'm not sure," I said, shaking my head as if to clear it. "I was angry. We had become—" I paused. "Almost . . . friends. If these were Manuel's men who had stolen from my neighbors and from my own father, I wanted to know it. I wanted to know how much he was part of it."

It was Almonzo's turn to shake his head. "You are your father's son, Harvey," he said. "That one thing is certain."

I thought this a strange thing for Almonzo to say, but it brought me square back to the issue.

"Where is Father?" I asked Alicia. She glanced up at Almonzo.

"Your father is at the house," he said softly. "And so are the others. They're holding a meeting about the Villistas."

"Right here? Right now?" I put my hand up to my head. "Is Father worried about me?" I asked Alicia. "Or is he angry?"

"A little of both, I'm afraid, " she answered.

"Well, I'd better go in there."

"Would you like me to come with you?" Almonzo asked.

I couldn't help grinning. "You bet I would! But I have to do this myself, don't I?" He nodded and smiled. "You can handle it, Harvey."

I walked to the house and in through the front door, expecting to come face to face with the men, but the parlor was empty. *They must be back in Father's office,* I thought. I hesitated. *What should I do now? Walk boldly in or wait for a summons?*

The clucking sound should have warned me, but I was too preoccupied to notice. Before I knew it Aunt Clair's arms were wound tightly around me, and I was clutched to her ample bosom and smothered with kisses.

"Harvey is home!" she announced in a voice of rapture. "Didn't I tell you? Didn't I say, 'That boy has pluck and good sense'—didn't I say that, Cleo?"

"You did," Aunt Cleo beamed. "I must go tell Leah."

"I'm right here." My mother's voice sounded sweet as music to me! I wriggled out of Aunt Clair's arms, fighting the urge to bury my head against my mother's slender, sweet-smelling shoulder.

She did it for me. She came over and put her arms around me and pulled me gently to her. I have always wondered how someone so frail could have so much strength. It was as if her own peace and fortitude flowed through me, releasing the built-up tensions of my long night. In a few moments she drew back and held me at arm's length, her hands resting lightly on my shoulders.

"The men are holding a meeting in your father's office," she said. "Did you know that?"

I nodded. "I've been out to the barn. Almonzo told me."

A wisp of a smile lifted the corners of her mouth. "Well, son," she said, "your father's instructions are that I bring you to him the moment you arrive. Are you up to that, Harvey?"

I wondered fleetingly what she would do if I answered no. "Yes, Mother," I said. "I'm all right. I'll go with you."

She took my hand and we walked out of the room together. When we reached my father's office, she knocked on the door, then released my hand and stood back.

"What is it, Leah?" my father's voice came.

"Harvey is here," she said. "Go on inside," she told me.

The smile in her blue eyes was the last thing I saw as I turned the handle. It was harder to enter that

room than it ever had been to enter the cave. I
stepped inside and shut the door softly behind me.
There was an empty chair waiting next to my father.
"Have a seat, Harvey," he said. I sat down beside
him. The room was silent, and everyone's eyes were
on me. I glanced around. The men gathered here were
neighbors, fathers of my friends, respected business-
men and Church leaders—I knew them all well. I
could sense the seething emotions so uneasily held in
check, suspended by this interruption.

"It is my understanding," my father began, "that
you might know something of what is going on
around here. Is that true, Harvey?"

I took a deep breath. "If you mean, do I know
something of the activity of the Villistas, yes, Father."

There was emotion in my father's face, but I
couldn't read it.

"I have spoken with your sister, with Almonzo,"
he hesitated just slightly, "and with Rafael. I want a
full explanation from you. Do you understand,
Harvey?"

I glanced at the men. I had thought their presence
would make this easier, but it seemed to be making it
harder. I was on trial in front of witnesses. I began.

"It all started Monday night when some of us
boys played *Run, Sheep, Run.*" I saw one or two nods
of men whose sons had been there, who had probably
heard stories of my unsportsmanlike behavior.

"You all know how the game goes. Well, I was
one of the sheep. I hid down by the river." I hesitated.
I could go back step by step, feeling by feeling. But
they probably wanted just the straight, plain facts,

quickly given. "A wounded man, a Villista, caught
me and held a knife to my ribs, and forced me to help
him up to the caves. He would hide there, he said, 'til
his men came for him."

"Why didn't you go straight to your father with
what happened, young man?" a voice demanded. I
looked up. I should have known Brother Madder
would ask that. He was a clerk in one of the local
banks. He did everything by the books, but he didn't
have any sons. In fact, he wasn't yet married.

"I wanted to do that, believe me," I answered.
"But he had a gun—and that very long knife."

"It seems to me that a group of men could have
handled one outlaw, Harvey." Brother Jacobs spoke
softly, but his eyes were sharp and unkind.

"There's only one narrow path to the caves," I
reminded him patiently. "Anyone watching can see
every inch of that pathway. Someone would have
been hurt, maybe killed."

"Several have been hurt, and much property lost
because of that outlaw, Harvey!" Brother Jacob's
voice was growing as angry as his eyes. "Because he
was here, this is where his friends struck. If he'd been
elsewhere—or dead!"

I turned to my father. "It wasn't that simple!
Manuel knew who you were. He knew who we all
were. He threatened to kill you and Mother and even
Alicia."

My father fixed Brother Jacobs with one of his
severe, you-are-out-of-line looks. Brother Jacobs
dropped his eyes.

"If you recall, brethren, I asked Harvey to give

me, to give us, a full explanation. He cannot do that if he is constantly interrupted." He turned back to me, his eyes incredibly kind and tender. "Continue, Harvey. Please."

"Tuesday night I went back as he told me to with food and water. The next night after the community meeting, I went again. He said it wouldn't be long 'til his friends came for him. Last night, you remember, Father, the calf was born. There was no chance for me to break away and go up there."

Had that been only last night—less than twenty-four hours before? It seemed days and years since then!

"I was worried about what Manuel might do when I didn't show up. So today during lunch I snuck away from school and headed up to the cave. But I didn't make it past the bridge. Lewis Palmer stopped me."

I glanced at Brother Palmer. He had leaned a bit forward in his chair. "Almonzo sent him after me, and you know how stubborn Lewis can be." Brother Palmer nodded. "So I went back to school with him. Then you know what happened. When the banditos struck, the principal dismissed school and sent us all home."

"Did you come straight here?" my father asked.

"Yes. Helena met me. She was in hysterics because the Villistas had taken Starfire and Alicia had gone after him."

My father's face seemed to pale a little. Was it possible that he might not know this part of the story?

"Tell me quickly what happened, Harvey," he demanded.

I told him. He seemed to hang on my words, but he showed no other reaction. I took him through the time of my accusations against Rafael and my leaving. I told him about entering the cave, about my confrontation with Juan and the other men who had stolen Starfire. I told him what happened when Rafael came. And I told him of sitting cross-legged on the serapes and eating Mormon chickens with the Villistas.

Then I stopped. The men looked at one another. The silence grew long. I coughed, then swallowed.

"They let the boy go," Brother Johnson said lamely.

"They know better than to kill a boy," Brother Dobson countered. "That means nothing." A babble of voices rose and swelled.

"They might not be ready to kill yet, but they will be. . ." "If they get away with theft and destruction Scot-free, you can bet they'll go further. . ." "It will never end until we end it. . ." "Let the word spread that the Mormon colonies are easy prey, and what chance have we then? . . ."

I couldn't keep track of what was said or who said it. For every word spoken in favor of patience and peace there seemed half a dozen in favor of action. I had never heard these men talk this way, with these voices and faces. For the first time that day I was truly frightened. I looked at my father. He made no move to control them. The talk went around and around and around in a vain, vicious circle. At last he held up his hand, and the speaking subsided. He spoke to me without turning his face or his eyes in my direction.

"Harvey," he asked, "did you happen to hear any of the Villistas make a statement concerning their future plans?"

I didn't answer. He turned then and looked at me sharply. "There have been rumors and wild boasts here. Did you hear it also? Did the Villistas want to headquarter in these caves? Use this as some sort of central bivouac or encampment?"

I shivered involuntarily. I saw the lady's sightless eyes and the point of her blade. "There is no chance of that, Father," I said. "They may have had notions, but I don't think that is their desire now."

"He doesn't think! What does the boy know?" Brother Jacobs muttered.

I stood up. "These men are not vicious murderers," I said. "They are patriots. If we deal with them justly—"

"Oh, yes, by all means, like they dealt with us! Without my team I can't drive into town to buy my supplies, boy. Without my oxen I can't plow my fields and plant my seed or harvest the crop that's my only living—"

"I didn't mean that, I didn't mean that at all," I said lamely. "I just don't think we should fight or kill them."

"I say we storm the caves right now," Brother Jacobs urged. "They'll be in a drunken sleep you can bet—they won't expect us."

I took a few steps toward my father, then froze. The men froze, too; they had all heard it. The stamping of many horses. I went to the window. Perhaps Manuel saw the curtain move. I don't think he saw my face. He cupped his hands around his mouth. "Harvey!" he shouted. "Harvee." The word trailed off into eerie silence. My father walked to my side. "Are these the men you have told us about?" he asked. I nodded. "I will go speak to them," he said. "No, Father," I protested. "Please, let me talk to him. Manuel won't hurt me. It will dishonor me in his eyes if I let someone else go in my place—even my father."

There were a few scoffs and murmurs from the men, but I noticed that no one but my father volunteered to go face the Villistas.

My father searched my face for a long, tense moment. "All right, Harvey," he said. "But I will be right behind you. If you sense any trouble, raise your arm up high. I will see it."

I walked from the room and past my mother, who watched me pale-eyed. I went out and into the yard where the mounted Villistas waited.

Chapter Sixteen

Several of the men on horseback carried torches. It was easy to spot Manuel. The horse he rode was a tall one, and it stood a little apart from the others. As I approached I saw that he wore his new sombrero and a bandelero full of bullets slung over his shoulder. He looked a little fierce, or at least all business. From the corner of my eye, I saw Almonzo standing in the square of light from the open barn door. Manuel's grave features lit up with a smile when he saw me.

"Harvey, my friend, I have come to say goodbye."

I craned my neck and looked into his face. "You are really going?"

He crossed himself. "*¡Barbaridades!* Do you think we would stay now?" He laughed out loud: "You do good work, my little gringo. And you are a *magnifico soldado*—a very brave soldier."

"So are you, Manuel," I said. "I think I shall miss you."

He looked me over, and his eyes grew solemn. "I am glad to hear this. I will miss you also." His lips parted in a grin. "Pobrecito, what will you do for excitement?"

I grinned back. "This will last me awhile, I think!"

He nodded and laughed again. He liked that answer. Suddenly he turned half-around in the saddle and lifted his hand in a quick, short gesture. I felt a tension tighten my muscles. What was he doing? Juan and two other men rode forward, then on and past Manuel to the end of the long drive that led into our property.

"What are they doing, Manuel?" I asked.

"Be patient, gringo. What a bother you are with your endless questions!"

Long minutes passed before I saw the shape of the men reappearing. Then I realized there were more than just three animals coming. I heard my father come out onto the porch. The same fears were with him. Was this some easy, quiet ambush Manuel had planned?

"You still do not trust me, Harvey," Manuel said. "I am sorry to see that." He turned to face the front of the house. "Señor Hales," he called out. "Would you do me the honor of speaking with me?"

I heard my father coming. I didn't dare turn to face him. I kept my eyes on Manuel's face. I saw nothing to fear there.

By the time my father reached the Villistas the mounted men were closer, near enough for me to see that they drove a sizeable bunch of animals before them: horses, cattle, a small herd of goats that were loudly complaining.

Manuel made a graceful, sweeping gesture with his arm. "My compliments, señor," he said to my father. "You have a son I would be proud to call my own."

My father made a slight bow. "It is true, what you say," he replied. "Gracias, señor."

Manuel gave an answering nod. "Harvey saved

my life," he continued. "And he dealt honorably with me." He threw back his head. His band of bullets shimmered silver in the glow of the torches. "A good Villista returns honor for honor," he cried. "So I return to you the animals my men have taken!"

He flicked his hand, and the three men herded the horses and cattle into the circle of light where my father could see them.

"Have your men move them into the small enclosure behind the barn. They will be safe there for now," my father instructed.

Manuel flicked his hand, and his men obeyed him. I stole a glance at my father. How calm he was in his boldness! Manuel leaned down in his saddle and began talking rapidly to my father. It would take his men some time to complete the task he had given them. *Did I dare do the thing I was thinking of? Did I have time?*

I walked closer to Manuel and my father. "Excuse me," I shouted. *"Espérame*—I will be back in a very few minutes." My father glanced at me questioningly, but Manuel nodded. "Don't go anywhere!" I called back over my shoulder.

I ran into the house past my startled aunts and the watching brethren. Once in my room I reached for the book. It was where I had left it. The leather cover felt cool and familiar against my fingers. *Paper— where was some paper?* I reached for my school books. My fingers were trembling and my mind wouldn't settle itself into thought.

"Estimada María," I wrote on the white surface. *What could I say in such a short space of time?*

"I send this gift," I began, "by the hand of your husband." I wrote rapidly for several minutes, with no leisure to think out the words, but only to feel them. I folded the paper, slipped it inside the book, and then ran outdoors.

They were still there! I had had a feeling they all might vanish. Manuel had leaned over, listening carefully to something my father was saying. The three men were back in the ranks, sitting tall on their horses. All were in order and ready to go. They were waiting for me.

I walked over to Manuel and thrust out the book. His dark eyes narrowed. "What is this?"

"It is for María," I said.

A look came over his face that I remembered from that first night when I read her letter. He reached for the book, then held it up so the light could touch it. He traced with his finger the Spanish written along the spine.

"El Libro de Mormón—the Book of Mormon," I said out loud.

"In Spanish?" He raised an eyebrow. I nodded.

"The book is rare in Spanish," I said. "It is my own copy. I would like María to have it, please."

Manuel ran a finger along his cheek. "This is a big gift to give, gringo. Are you certain?"

"Very certain," I replied, meeting his eyes.

He smiled, but the smile was strangely lopsided. "Very well." He thrust the book down into the leather bag slung over his saddle. "I shall take good care of your book, Harvey. María will be very pleased."

I stood back. The horses stamped and began to

move now. "Where will you go?" I called.

Manuel grinned this time. "Here and there, wherever the wind leads us. Our horses are fresh, and our bandaleros are fat with bullets."

"And you are anxious to fight," I said, without thinking.

Manuel spurred his horse and pulled at the reins, so the animal danced in place. "There is much work for a revolutionary to do. Sí, Harvey?"

"Sí, Manuel," I replied. "Vaya con Dios."

He paused, it seemed in mid-air. His black eyes swept me. "Manuel will give the last gift, Harvey," he cried. He drew the long gleaming knife from its sheath and tossed it upward, where its surface caught fire from the torches so that it, too, was a glowing brand. He reached up and caught it, then threw it again in a gentle arc toward me. I watched the circling blade intently until my fingers closed safely around the handle.

"While you have the knife you will not forget Manuel, sí?" the Villista cried.

He turned in one graceful sweep, and his men turned with him. I watched them thunder down the lane. "Sí, Manuel," I said softly. The pounding of their horses throbbed like a rhythm inside my head.

Indistinctly, as though in a dream, I saw Alicia grab Almonzo's hand and race toward me. Through swimming eyes I saw the porch fill up with my father's friends. I saw my mother, her sweet gentle face framed in the yellow halo of her hair. But the only thing I saw clearly was my father—and the look in his eyes as he reached for my hand.

Susan Evans McCloud is most well known as an LDS novelist, although her previously published writings include poems, feature articles for an Illinois newspaper, narratives for tapes and filmstrips, screenplays, including the award-winning *John Baker's Last Race, The Gift* and the stage version of *Charlie's Monument.* Her lyrics published and recorded, include two hymns in the 1985 LDS hymn book: *Lord, I Would Follow Thee* and *As Zion's Youth in Latter-days.* With the publication of *Black Stars Over Mexico,* she has taken a significant step into the field of children's literature.

The author, a niece of Joseph Fielding and Jesse Evans Smith, was born in Utah and raised there and in Illinois. She and her husband, James, have six children and five grandchildren. Her only son plays the bagpipes and Susan is much involved in Celtic studies, music and history. The family, dwindled to two remaining daughters, a Sheltie and a Yorkshire Terrier, resides in Provo, Utah.